The Boy

Who Walked

A Way

Nancy Janes

The Boy Who Walked A Way
Copyright ©2012 Nancy Janes
jazele@live.com

Images: Courtesy of Big stock photos
Book Cover design: Heather Randall & Nancy Zelman

ISBN : 1479139076
ISBN 13 : 9781479139071
LCCN : 2012915139

CreateSpace Independent Publishing Platform
North Charleston, South Carolina

Preface

There is a land in dreamtime where happiness is a state of being. The sunshine falls in radiant showers, and the rains fall in gentle sprays upon an earth that offers its cornucopia of gifts freely. The trees grow tall and straight, with leaves so green they shimmer like silk when the soft winds blow through them. The land is fragrant with flowers that are gowned in beauty, scenting the air with sweetness.

The seas and streams of water run pure and clear and gladden the heart of all living creatures. The birds of the air and the animals of the ground share space with the earth's inhabitants in cooperative friendship. All creation rejoices in quiet benediction in its creatures that are at peace.

Come—unleash your sense of wonder and belief. Put on your hiking boots, and hit the trail with Jal on an expedition to the peaceable kingdom.

For my mother, Erie,
who has immigrated to Syntee's country.

The story of Jal is dedicated to all who seek the ideal country
and labor with the Great
High King to bring it into being.

...For he looked for a city...
—Hebrews 11:10 (KJV)

Prologue

In the twentieth century, a long struggle ended in the subjugation of a malevolent enemy. Following this event, a confederation of nations, based upon a Constitution for a United World, came into being. Subsequently, an unprecedented age of peace began, founded on humanistic principles. Harmony reigned among the member states for several generations. Then a number of rogue nations pulled out of the confederation. Negotiations failed to restore the balance of power. In or about 2146, a repressive regime triggered an attack on a neighboring country. Warfare, once set in motion, rapidly spun out of control. One by one the nations were drawn into the fray.

The principal country of the World Confederation HQs, which had been neutral for several years, entered the conflict in 2162. And here our story begins.

Amid the chaos of war, a young boy, Jal Valyhn, struggles to survive. Alone and helpless, bereft of his loved ones, he has an encounter with an unseen being that leads to a seven-days journey. Accompanied by two appointed guides, he sets out for a safe haven. And here is the cue for your entrance dear reader.

First Day

1

Beneath the canopy of a large willow tree, a slight form blended into the shadows of the night. As the darkness lightened to silvered hues of gray, the form assumed the contours of a young boy in restless sleep. The dawn passed; above the horizon, the sun, resplendent in streamers of crimson, tinted the tree in a roseate glow. Sunlight gleaming through the leaves fell upon the boy's tear-streaked face. He moved his head to shut out the brightness, and then, with a fitful sigh and a muffled, "Uncle Joulh," he abruptly opened his eyes and sat up. Lifting his dusty hands, he wiped his face, leaving smudges from his chin to his forehead.

Puzzled by his surroundings, he stood upright and inspected the dense foliage that encircled him on every side. The noise of swishing and gurgling water attracted his attention, and he turned to note the source. A stream was running parallel to the willow tree, and one thickly leafed bough was trailing back and forth in the slow-moving water. On the far side of the stream, a swan breezing along on a small pond stopped and stared at the tree. The boy wondered idly what the object of interest could be as he began to brush the grass and twigs from his clothes.

All at once, the roiling tremors at the back of his mind surfaced in overwhelming waves. He leaned against the trunk of the tree and bit by bit slipped to the ground. He pulled his legs up to his chest, put his head on his knees, and wept in utter misery. Wrenching sobs shook his body as he murmured under his breath, "Uncle Joulh, I have to find Uncle Joulh."

The night's search that had stranded him under the willow tree shuffled through his memory in disjointed fragments and merged with the quest for his parents six months earlier. Images began to flip through his mind like a slide show. Unmoored from time and place, he was home again reliving the days prior to his parents' entry into the military.

He awoke at his usual hour on that ill-fated morning. The sunshine pouring into his room gave promise of a pleasant day ahead. Snippets of conversation floated up the stairs. *Dad hasn't left for work yet. My birthday is tomorrow, not today,* he thought, as he bounded out of bed. Rushing through his shower, he dressed and ran downstairs. On his entrance to the kitchen, his parents ceased speaking. "Good morning, dear," his mother said in a restrained tone. He halted in midstep and looked at his father. Then he noted his mother's subdued expression.

"What's the matter, Mom? Is anything wrong? What are you and Dad talking about?"

"Your father will tell you after breakfast, Jal. We'll eat in the dining room. Your favorite is coming right up."

Jal sat at the table, tearing his beloved cherry crepe into pieces with his fingers. Each bite felt like a leaden pellet dropping into his stomach. He dawdled as long as possible while his parents chatted and waited patiently for him to finish.

"Jal, pay attention, please." His mother's voice filtered through his mutinous thoughts. "I've said Neilh and I will both be home for your birthday tomorrow."

He scowled, ignored her remarks, and put his plate to the side. "Mom, what do you want to tell me?"

"We received news this morning that affects us all, my dear. Nielh will share it with you."

He avoided the eyes of his father, with a heartfelt longing to defer the talk he dreaded.

"What is it, Mom?"

Nielh pushed his chair from the table. "That's enough, son. Let's go to the study."

Jal picked up his fork. "Okay, Dad, in a tic. I haven't finished my crepe." He stalled, wishing he had asked for two crepes instead of just one.

"Please, excuse us, Syrah," Nielh said and then stood up. "Jal, come with me this instant," he said in a stern voice, walking from the room.

"Obey your father, dear," Syrah said. "Don't keep him waiting."

With a sense of foreboding, Jal got to his feet and left the room. On reaching the doorway of the study, he said, "Just a sec, Dad; my hands need washing."

He eked out a few more minutes until his father spoke in an impatient voice. "Now, son! I mean now!"

His supply of stalling techniques exhausted, he answered, "Okay, Dad," and entered the study.

Nielh sat behind his desk, as if wishing to distance himself from the words he had to say. He bowed his head for a moment and then looked at Jal with troubled eyes. "Early this morning, Syrah and I received a dispatch from the Defense Office. There is no ignoring the orders to report for duty.

"Our country has been at war for the past six months—a war we didn't want. Nonetheless, it happened anyway. So here we are. Our civic obligations are clear-cut. Your studies on the subject have taught you that; you need no refresher on the topic."

Jal, silent to this point, blurted out, "What is this, Dad? I don't want to hear it!"

"You must hear, son. The time for not hearing is past. This morning we received orders from the Office of Defense to report for service duties within the week. It is imperative to link each branch of the military to a secure systems network. Syrah and I are the coordinators of the project, and we'll be traveling nonstop until the work is completed. It troubles us deeply, but we have no other recourse than to leave you in the care of your uncle."

Jal listened to his father's words with increasing anxiety. He stood up and slammed his open palm on the desktop. "No! No, Dad. You can't go; I won't let you go."

"Sit down and control yourself, Jal. Several times, you've wished that you could fight a dragon and defeat it. Why, you said it to your uncle less than a week ago! Well, a real dragon is facing us now—the biggest one there is."

Jal's mother came into the room and took his hand. "My dear. Please…"

Heedless, Jal snatched his hand from hers and glared at his father with compressed lips. "I don't want to fight any old dragon; I want you and Mom to stay here." He stormed about the house in a rage, crying out repeatedly, "You can't go; I won't let you go."

His frenzy lasted for hours. In mid-afternoon, worn out from the tempest within, he subsided into a restive sleep.

He awoke in the night and with stifled sobs went over the day's events with obsessive intent. *They can't go; I won't let them. It's the fault of that group.*

Fully engaged in his studies, he had ignored the scores of adults who met daily in his home. Transient scraps of their conversations drifted through his mind during the progression of his happy days. *What do they mean? A war...what war?*

Though he was aware of the participants dwindling, he asked no questions while the weeks went by. He avoided any reference to the war, as if he intuitively knew of the coming disruptions to his life. When his mother introduced the subject of possible military service, Jal refused to listen. "No, Mom, I don't want to hear this."

She would sigh, "Jal, there's no way to avoid it. We have to talk."

He foiled her attempt to speak on several occasions by making excuses. "Not right now, Mom. Sorry, we'll talk later." Or "Uhlin and Lonah are here. We're studying for a test." In the evenings, he put her off by going to his room. "I'm so sleepy, Mom. Tell me tomorrow."

Due to the uncertain timing of her and Nielh's military induction, Syrah didn't press Jal to talk.

One evening, Jal overheard his mother say, "Time enough, Nielh." His father looked at her with loving eyes and upraised eyebrows. Then he continued to pen a memo to his office staff for the next day. Jal snuck behind their backs and ran upstairs to his room.

At length, weary with thoughts of the past events preceding his troubled day, he dropped off to sleep and to dream.

Fierce dragons were busily devouring the tree in which he was hiding when he felt a silky touch on his face.

"Uncle Joulh is here," his mom said. "Time to wake up, my birthday boy."

Jal opened his eyes, saw his uncle in the doorway, and jumped out of bed to hug him.

"Good morning, Jal. Happy tenth year on this April 12, 2162: a momentous birthday."

"Thank you, Uncle Joulh. You will stay for the whole day, won't you?"

"Nothing could keep me away. Your admission to the IGM, and birthday—a double celebration. We'll go to the Natural History Museum—our most fun outing."

"I was hoping that we might go; a topping idea, Uncle Joulh. A ripping good time."

After showering and dressing, Jal ate his breakfast in silence while his mother and uncle finalized plans for the day.

"We'll have lunch at your favorite cafe today, Jal. Cake and ice cream are an after-dinner treat. I didn't forget, love," his mother said.

"First the fun, later the dessert, Mom. I hope the cake is chocolate for Uncle Joulh and me."

"A confidential detail, my love. The U tube is waiting; let's go."

The diversions of the morning and the afternoon proved to be magical remedies of healing. Beguiled by the museum's exhibits, Jal forgot his ordeal of the previous day. Their late lunch at the outdoor cafe complemented their museum tour. The special family dinner and birthday gifts, including chocolate cake and ice cream, filled the evening hours. *I'll be strong like Dad*, Jal said to himself that night as he reviewed the day's pleasing activities.

Early the next morning, Jal's resolve in the night evaporated as he grasped the reality of his mother's words. "My love, support is critical to our country's survival. We may resist to the uttermost, yet it can't rid us of the job we have to do. A year isn't so very long; it might seem forever to you, but the months will pass. Think of Uhlin living with his grandfather, Cousin Tabor. His parents are serving in the military. Still, he seems happy enough. Joulh is our cherished stand-in member in all circumstances like Cousin Tabor is for Uhlin."

"Why do you say that, Mom?"

"Why, Jal? Because Nielh was five years old when Joulh became his caregiver at the age of eighteen. Arah and Litha, their dad and mom, were lost at sea. They loved sailing and spent their leisure time navigating the coastal islands. They were celebrating their twentieth anniversary when a sudden, horrific storm swept their boat out to sea. The details of the accident are unknown. Joulh was the mainstay of strength for Neilh then and remains so for our family. My parents died in a viral epidemic when I was two years old. My only living relative, Aunt Euna, perished in another virus outbreak before you were born. It's the same infection that's prevented by a vaccine nowadays."

"I was wondering about our family, Mom. Uhlin's grandfather is Cousin Tabor. I don't have any grandparents. A cousin is different from an uncle, Mom."

"Yes, Tabor was cousin to your grandfather and his business partner. The aid and comfort he gave to Joulh and Nielh during the time of their unbearable loss is beyond measure. Cousin Tabor is a valued friend and family member.

"Save your questions about family members for later. Let's concentrate on our subject: your uncle loves you dearly and will move in here with you. How pleased he was at your birth. 'At long last, a nephew,' he said. 'And stuck with the name, Joulh—thanks to my only brother and his lovely wife.' He announced your birth to everyone in the village and aired it by the public newscaster. My love, his help is essential if we are to endure our separation.

"Somehow, we have to accept the things we can't change, and this is one of them. Never forget that we're in this together.

The motto of the Valhyns is, 'Forward to victory.' In the meantime, your father and I will be home on leave in six weeks. Let's focus on planning outings for our break instead of being miserable wretches over things we can't control. With courage, my love, we'll make the best of this unhappy situation."

"I want to be courageous and victorious with you and Dad, Mom. Why can't I go with you? How do I know you won't be out on a sailboat?"

"Children aren't permitted to accompany parents. We might by chance run across dangerous situations during the year, but it won't be on a sailboat. Our work will be within specific safe areas of the military."

She held him in her embrace and said, "Love isn't always easy, Jal. Sometimes its demands are almost unbearable. My dear, how I wish it could be different."

Jal, lacking his usual animation, moved listlessly through the following days. When he and his mother discussed their coming separation, he sought to reassure her. "Don't worry, Mom. Uncle Joulh and I will be okay. Time will race by, just as you said."

The succeeding days were filled with the tasks necessary for an extended absence. Jal, excused from his studies, stayed close to his parents under a pretense of being helpful. His mother kept an anxious eye on him while she maintained their normal household routine. On their last evening together, she made his favorite meal of fish and chips.

Before he went off to bed, Jal said, "Thanks, Mom; I'll be your chef for breakfast when you get home. We'll go to the musical arcade and have lunch at our favorite outdoor café. That's what we'll do."

"That's a promise, my dear," Syrah said.

The next morning, as Jal's parents left to take up their duties in the military, his mother recapped their agreement. "Recite to me your to-do list while we're away, Jal."

"Be sure I keep up with my lesson plans and don't neglect my language studies," he replied. "Allyn, our tutor, is on hand if our class has difficulty with any subject. I'm not to forget to help Uncle Joulh with the household chores."

"You're spot on," she said, holding him close in her embrace. "Your uncle has your schedule, and the agenda includes fun things with Uhlin and your other friends. We'll see you in six weeks, my love."

2

Unable to accept the fact of his parents' departure, Jal brooded during the morning and afternoon, *They may be in the village still. I'll go see if they are.* He sneaked away while his uncle was busy making dinner. He searched for them in the milling crowds, among the flood of refugees and the military personnel. At midnight, with all lights out and the streets deserted, he sat down on a curb to rest. Yielding to hunger and weariness, he slept undisturbed on the street pavement.

When Jal didn't show up to set the table for dinner, Joulh alerted Tabor. They searched for hours and located him at daybreak, still fast asleep on the pavement. Joulh carried him home, and later, after a much-needed rest, he said to Jal in a reassuring tone, "They had no choice but to go. We have to put up with many things we don't like at this time. You and I must do the best we can. Together, we'll get through these dreadful times."

Jal took a deep breath, brushed his tears away, and said, "I'm sorry, Uncle. I didn't mean to cause you trouble; I just miss them so."

After this incident, Jal sank into a glum silence, rarely smiling or chatting with his uncle. Joulh, involved with the tasks of everyday life, scheduled a time for casual chats. "Young man, we'll have a confab before you're off to bed. Brief me on the day's doings, and then we'll review your homework."

And so, Jal put aside his grief to share his activities with his uncle in the evenings.

The words of his mother as they said good-bye reeled through his mind each day: "The cord of love is strong, my dear. It threads its way from my heart to your heart no matter how distant we may be from each other." Lying in bed at night, he repeated the words to himself like a mantra.

Six weeks inched away—a time that seemed endless to Jal as he waited for his parents to arrive home on leave. They came at last, and their treasured days together sped by in a flurry of activities. Once they had gone, Jal resigned himself to their absence and carried on his studies with an occasional break with his friends. He resumed his mantra at night before falling asleep.

The ensuing interlude of peace ended when the war moved into his village. Four months after his parents' leave of absence, Jal and his uncle fled their home along with friends and neighbors. The enemy pressed forward, seizing more territory each day. Now in their third refuge, it seemed to Jal they were on the run continually—a perpetual packing and leaving. During the months of their forced wanderings, he had clung to his uncle and refused to leave his side. He had few objections to the changes in his life except for a wistful mention of his cousin Uhlin now and then.

In the present village, a safe haven for the past two months, an everyday routine restored a semblance of order to their lives. The three compact rooms at the local inn were comfortable, and former neighbors of theirs lived in close proximity, including Jal's tutor, Allyn. Accordingly, Jal took up his daily studies again.

The arrival of Tabor and his family added to his feelings of security. He and Uhlin studied together as before. Jal came home from an overnight stay with Uhlin one morning and said, "That was fun, Uncle Joulh. You must get tired of me hanging on to you day in and day out."

"Not tired, Jal, but it's helpful to confront our fears. Fears, if left to grow, kindle a flame that blights our every waking moment. I recollect the time that you and I first played the dragon game. Your father and I played it when he was your age. I tell you, as I told him; Fears can be ferocious dragons. You do well, my lad, to oppose the dragons."

"Dad said the same thing to me, Uncle Joulh. Did he learn it from you?"

"He may well have, Jal. Sensible boy, he was."

In mid-September, the military required Joulh to accept an overnight assignment. With his sense of confidence restored, Jal protested against having to stay with Tabor during his uncle's absence. "I'm a big boy; you can trust me. I'll ask Uhlin over for the night if I miss you too much. Please, Uncle Joulh, say yes."

In the course of the next three weeks, Jal stayed alone four nights. "I'm not so fearful now; I'm a Valhyn," he said to his uncle one morning.

"Jal, let me correct myself. I didn't mean to imply that we aren't to be afraid at times. I confess I'm scared stiff on occasion. We Valhyns face down the dragons, even if we are petrified. The best we can do is defy, resist, and defang them. Don't forget, in case you ever do feel the gripping tentacles of fear, my brave Valhyn nephew."

A week later, Jal stayed alone for two sequential nights. He thought of his uncle's words and quelled his feelings of fear, especially on the second night. Joulh came home in the early morning of the third day and gave minimal explanation for his absence. At last, seeing Jal's imploring eyes, he said, "Dear boy, my assignments are requiring more time. I can't take you with me; it's too risky. Since you prefer to stay alone rather than with Cousin Tabor, I relayed your wish to him. He's available at any time if you need him. Be sure to look in on him once or twice a day while I'm gone.

"Yesterday I had good news; my commanding officer informed me that my duties would end in two months or less.

We might be home by then. The latest report from our village came last night. Our troops are winning out and the enemy is in flight. We will celebrate liberation yet, my boy! When there seems no end to our struggle, we cope with one day at a time. It's a no-choice situation. Keep your plucky Valhyn spirit. "

"It seems to me, Uncle Joulh, there's a lot of 'no-choices' since this war started."

"Very true, Jal," he said with a smile.

On two occasions, Jal received mail from his parents. "From your mom and dad," Joulh said, handing him the first missive.

After reading the letter, Jal pestered his uncle for details of their location. "Why can't I be with them?"

"No, no, my dear boy," Joulh said in a tense voice. "It's too dangerous. You've been through this topic with your mom, and the answer is still the same. They work in an area of military operations that demands constant attention. Your presence would be an endless worry. Don't forget, your dad and mom will be with us in a few months. In the meantime, we'll make do and hold on to our hope—you no less than me."

Aware of his uncle's distress, Jal began to suppress his feelings. On receiving the next letter, he took it with a mere, "Thank you, Uncle Joulh."

During mid-October, his uncle came in from a shopping trip and said. "I'm home, Jal. We need to talk."

What now? Jal thought with a sinking feeling as he laid his assignment aside and went out. His uncle said, as he put the last of the items away, "Our special dinner for today has to be postponed. I'm sorry, 'no choice' again. I received orders less than an hour ago for an important assignment. Maybe a two-day task, but not more than three to complete—"

He broke off at Jal's interruption. "I'll help you cook a posh dinner when you get home, Uncle Joulh; this evening Uhlin and I can eat at the café next door. Don't worry about me."

"Good thinking, Jal. Please check in with Cousin Tabor every day. Do this favor for me and be polite when he calls on you. I'm sure Uhlin will be in and out; ask him to stay over-night if your zest for solitude wanes. I'll be home as soon as I can. The household money is in the right-hand desk drawer in case you need anything. Carry on, my lad."

Jal did carry on with his scheduled activities for two days. On the third day, troubled by a sense of dread, his anxiety intensified. Yet he refused Tabor's offers of help, and each morning's call in was met by the same reply: "I'm fine, Cousin Tabor. Don't bother about me."

Jal, on repeated occasions, rebuffed Uhlin's attempts to engage him in their usual afternoon board games. As a result, Uhlin seldom came by after their morning studies. He ignored Tabor's biddings to dinner and went out solely to buy the sparse food available. His growing uneasiness magnified his loneliness, as he lay awake nightly to a booming sound like thunder in the distance. From overhearing the villagers' gossip, he knew the enemy's approach was imminent.

On his fifth night alone, apprehensive and unable to sleep, Jal left the inn. He wandered up and down countless streets inquiring for news of his uncle. Past midnight, he found himself on the outskirts of the village. The crowds thinned; the road became a graveled path. A bit further, he spied the willow tree. Tired and frightened, he crept under the sheltering branches and sank into a fretful slumber. The same disturbing dream came, as it had repeatedly, since leaving his family home. He searched for his parents through unknown and dimly lit streets. He glimpsed them rounding a corner and ran to catch up, only to discover they were nowhere in sight.

3

Jal, recalled from his lengthy reverie by a sudden noise, sat up with an expectant air. He listened with indrawn breath, but only the sound of the gurgling and swishing water came to him. He saw through his tears the swan gliding on the pond and thought. *Oh, that I could be a swan, I would then be free from all my troubles.* As he wept, he grew conscious of movements. Suppressing his sobs, he noticed the branches of the tree lightly swaying.

He watched the swan emerge from the water and walk to the bank of the stream. Nearby, a multicolored butterfly, luminescent in the morning sun, settled on a leaf. He heard a muted noise like a knock and stood up to peer about for the source. He dropped his head aside to listen and picked up a whisper. "What is the cause, child? Why do you weep?"

Startled, Jal walked around the enclosed space and looked up. The early-morning sun interlaced the leaves with a blush and cast a reddish glimmer on the ground. The grasses on the far bank of the stream stirred, as if touched by a puff of air, and he heard the question repeated. He walked to the furthest perimeter of the tree and scrutinized its leafy pinnacle. *Someone is speaking...a voice....* The words were spoken a third time. "Why do you weep, my child?"

He took a step backward and stuttered out, "I'm so— so afraid. I can't find Uncle Joulh. He's been gone almost a week; I don't know what to do. I searched for him most of the night."

The insistent whisper came yet again, "Be comforted, my child. Do not fear; listen to my words."

Jal stood motionless and glanced about with a quick movement of his head. The swan was standing inside the tree enclosure with inquisitive eyes on him.

Perplexed, he pulled on his earlobe in distrust of his own hearing and felt a waft of air on his tear-drenched face. The incessant whisperer continued, "I am Simeon, the appointed Guardian of the South. I am the Keeper of all who hear my voice and obey my instructions. During the course of my appointed time, I have seen great troubles come and go in this land. Take note, Jal Valhyn, and consider my advice, if you are to escape the greater troubles yet to come."

My name...he knows that I'm Jal Valhyn. His eyes widened, and he brought his hands to his face at a complete loss for words. He inspected the area yet again. The swan was now standing near the butterfly, their eyes on him, as if listening to the conversation. Jal regarded them tensely. He said hesitantly, "What am I to do?"

"You must go to Grandfather Moutyn to gain the sanctuary you need. In safety and security, you will grow strong under his guidance. This morning you will begin your expedition."

"How am I to get to Grandfather Moutyn?" Jal said in a wail of dismay. "How am I to get there? Are you going with me?"

"No, my child, I am Simeon, the Appointed One. I remain in this place for a season. As I am appointed, I appoint others. I am Syntee to my messengers, and to the ones who obey my word. Bea and Sammie are the messengers who will go with you to Grandfather Moutyn."

In a moment's solemn stillness, Jal weighed the possibility of Bea and Sammie voicing the words. *Can a swan and a butterfly speak?*

"No, Jal, Sammie, and Bea aren't speaking; it is I, Syntee, addressing you. File my instructions in your memory; it is vital that you keep to the path running by the stream. Once across a wooden bridge, enticing music rings out in resonating peals in a flower-strewn meadow. A golden haze in swirling rainbow hues may appear to be in motion. Do not delay. Go past the meadow immediately.

"The path ascends higher, and you will come to a frozen plain, the home of the Icy Ones. Pass beyond briskly. Supplies for each day are sufficient, and a kind reception awaits you on the way. Be of good courage, Jal. Your uncle Joulh arrives home by mid-morning, and he knows that you are safe. So will your mom and dad. The message went out an hour ago." There was a long pause, and then Syntee said, "Bea and Sammie will give you further instructions as you travel. Go now, child! Grandfather Moutyn anticipates your arrival."

Jal scanned the enclosed space yet again for a visible presence; his eyes then rested on Sammie and Bea. *I feel like my whirligig when it's spinning. What am I to do?* Unmoving, he stood ruffling his hair with a mystified expression on his face as he examined the surroundings.

The fronds of the grass on the opposite side of the stream stirred, as if bowing to the gentle wind that rustled through them. The swishing and gurgling sounds became indistinct, and the pathway, clearly marked, stood out in bold relief. A mist resembling dew rose up from the ground, and a coolness touched his tear-streaked face.

Bea and Sammie, with their alert eyes on him waited, while minutes went by in his effort to make a decision. With an indrawn breath, his answer came, "Yes, I'll go now, Syntee."

"I'm Sammie, Jal. Bea and I will go with you to your new home. Our course is plotted, and off we go."

Bea, poised on Sammie's head, said, "Time this trio made tracks."

"Syntee," she said, "I got four T's in that sentence."

Jal caught a soft chuckle but no reply.

"Bea, no games. Reserve your play for homecoming," Sammie said in a firm voice. And he took a decisive step in the direction of the path.

"An expedition to revel in," he said to Syntee in a farewell wave.

"It is indeed, Syntee," Bea added.

Jal took one hesitant step and said in a tremulous tone, "Will I meet you again, Syntee?"

"We will meet again, Jal. And yes, I am real. Go now, child." Thoughts and feelings in disarray, Jal followed Sammie to the path that bypassed the village. *The booming was loud last night and getting louder. I'll have to leave anyway, so I might as well go with Bea and Sammie.* The words of Syntee came to him: "I am the Keeper of all who hear my voice and obey." His turbulent thoughts and misgivings lessened, and his steps quickened. Sammie's leisurely pace speeded up at the same time. Bea sat nimbly on his head, her eyes on Jal.

The path curved among the trees, and soon the village was behind them. Jal, mentally wrestling to make sense of his experience, became aware of a high-pitched whining noise.

"Here's the bridge we cross. I've said it three times," Bea yelled.

"Sorry, Bea. I'm in a fuddle."

In front of them, a bridge arched above the stream. Jal paused midway to look at the burbling water flowing over multi-colored stones. "How pretty. May I take one?"

Bea said, "No, Jal, the stones aren't ours to take. The pretty things belong to the stream, our friend and our teacher. It would be like taking its burblings away."

Jal continued to gaze at the translucent colored stones.

"Listen," he whispered. "A water song."

"Yes, the stream is singing," Sammie replied. "Do you get the tune?"

"The sounds are like a lyric!" Jal exclaimed. "I do so want to learn what the stream can teach me. Maybe you two can help me, Sammie. Do you think you might?"

Bea flew to his shoulder. "We'll be happy to help you, but the best teacher is the stream itself. As you quietly listen to its song, you'll learn most. So be patient, Jal."

They stepped off the bridge into a narrow path bounded by a petite meadow and rimmed by a grove of trees. A ground covering of wildflowers filled the open spaces.

"I didn't see the meadow from the bridge. How did it appear from out of the blue like this? Do you know, Sammie?"

"Not so mysterious, Jal, or is it? The design of the bridge is the enigma. Once we step in the meadow, it becomes obvious. But don't ask me how and why. The frame of the bridge is hardly visible from here. We're as baffled as you are each time we come this way. Now, about the meadow—for some reason, Bea and I are immune to its special effects. We help others resist the strange power. That's why Syntee instructs us to hustle over. Our lacks on the subject leave us nothing else to tell you, Jal. We'll wait and learn with you."

Entranced, Jal viewed the meadow as a drama and refrained from further questions. *Like the play Mom and I went to last summer, but 3-D,* he thought.

The flowers made an extravagant display in brilliant tones of blue, purple, and yellow. A low, pleasant humming sound began to vibrate and imbue the air in a swirling, shimmering rainbow. The meadow, suffused with misty droplets of a saffron-colored haze, appeared to be in motion. Jal, mesmerized by the beauty, moved toward the variegated colors.

"No, Jal," Sammie said tersely. "We're not to stop here!"

"Absolutely not!" Bea stated in alarm, brushing Jal's face with a wing.

Sammie took his hand and tugged him back to the path. Diverted by Bea, settling again on Sammie's head, Jal lagged behind to view the furling of her wings. *Bea's the color of the flowers, but shimmery like the swirly colors in the air.* He kept staring at her as they hastened their pace over the meadow. *Wait until I tell Dad! He'll never believe it.*

A voice broke into his thoughts. "Wake up," Bea was saying loudly. "Control to station; do you receive us? Hijacker… abductor of thoughts? Which?"

"I'll tell you some time. Not right now, you—"

Sammie cut in. "Quiet, you two, let me speak. We'll cross the stream here at this shallow spot. Also, you can wash your face." He gestured to Jal's streaky face with a smile.

Jal took his shoes off, remarking their thin soles. *Not shoes for trekking,* he thought as he picked them up and waded into the water. Bea, from her safe perch, eyed him complacently while they crossed to the other side.

"No use to look at me so smugly from up there," Jal said drily.

"Wading in the water is fun. Isn't it, Sammie?"

"Great fun, Jal. Long legs are helpful," he replied.

"My nerves are getting frayed. Watch yourselves," Bea snapped.

Jal washed his face, put his shoes on, and realized the meadow seemed to be receding into the far distance. *Like an illusion. No use to ask the reason for the optic,* he said to himself. He began to inspect the location in front of them. On the left, a broad path with a smooth surface branched off from the stream. "Shall we go this way, Sammie?" He said with a sweeping gesture to the broad path.

"Never, Jal." Sammie replied. "That road is off limits and kaput to us. Syntee ordered us to always, but always stay on the path running by the side of the stream. The broad path is like an access road and leads to Daganland. We are never to set foot in Daganland; it is the Nitecraulers' native realm. Their way of life is the opposite of ours. They love the darkness and the moon as we love the day and the sun.

"Daganland's architecture is wacky and wondrous to us. We know because Bea and I once chanced a visit, and I can tell you, we never chanced another! Disobedience went by the wayside. The inhabitants of Daganland are aggressive and fixated on making trouble for others. The darkness in which they live inhibits their actions in the luminous quality of our country—I mean the country we are in at present. But they are ruthless in carrying out specialty operations in the countries of the world."

"They must be busy operating in the war then," Jal commented wryly.

"That, you can count on," Sammie said. "A stockpile of trivia to allay curiosity is in the offing at destination's end. The Nitecraulers are one big bundle of woe. Our hair-raising adventure, or more precisely a feather-raising one, taught us respect for Syntee's instructions. No need for a further demonstration for these two weasels."

Bea interrupted, "Smashing epic postponed. Hey! Put our weaslings on ice, Sammie."

"What a handsome fellow you are with a clean face, Jal. Follow me to the path," she said.

Jal stood motionless and stared at her wide-eyed. He said tartly, "You mean follow Sammie!"

"No," Bea said in a jesting tone. "I mean follow me."

"Cut it out, you two," Sammie said in a firm tone.

"Obey the boss!" Bea said and rapped him on the head.

Sammie rolled his eyes at Jal and walked on.

4

The path swerved inward toward the stream and widened into a steep upper slant as they went higher. Puffing from the climb, Jal took in the blue of the sky through the heavily leafed trees. The sun tipped the treetops, scattering dancing sunbeams on the path. *Like I'm walking on a ray of sunlight.* The leaves in hues of green with edgings of coral and red drew his attention. *The sun brushed them with its colors of the morning. Mom's favorite poem.* Hope and a feeling of trust welled up within him. Tears came to his eyes at the memory of his night's distress.

Bea perched upon his shoulder. "Whatever is the matter, Jal?" she said in a fluttery voice.

Sammie slowed his steps. "Tears, Jal? Tell us why the tears."

"I can't help crying, I'm so grateful to Syntee for you both. I've been so scared and lonely too."

Bea shook her head as Sammie said, "Syntee is truly a matchless being. We're glad He assigned you to us."

Jal dabbed at his eyes. "Would you tell me about Syntee and how you came to know him?"

"Sure, we will. Bea likes to recite first."

"Sammie and I do see eye to eye on that." She seated herself on his head. "We've been together for a long time, Jal. Maybe Sammie doesn't agree, but it seems so to me.

"The willow tree was the site of my birth and is still my home. The tangy blooms I love grew by the pond—lots of them. No worry about food. I was happy and contented with my life until the flowers began to wither in a summer drought. The fragrant delicacies of my diet wilted first. Only the coarser greenery remained. I tried one and then another. I even sampled some of the grasses that grew on the bank of the pond. They tasted worse than the plants.

"Discouraged, I moped around the house, getting hungrier by the day. In desperation, I ventured farther out beyond the pond in search of the sweet-scented plants. Fruitless searching it was, too. One miserable day I pitched into a grumbling fit on the unfairness of everything.

"Through the growing volume of my griping came a whisper. 'Having a pity party, are you? Feeling sorry for yourself, are you?' My eyes flared open, and my antennae went straight up. I thought they were going to fly off my head. I pulled my wings to my body in a fright, gasping and stuttering, 'Who…who are you?' I flew up and down and round the tree a dozen times trying to find the source of the words.

"I heard chuckling, and my alarm bell went into overdrive. 'Give up, Bea? Ready to listen?' Me oh my—I was not only ready but wiped out. I nearly toppled out of the tree; I clung tight to the branch and concentrated on the voice. Bushed and beat, I hung on to a branch mumbling to myself, 'You've lost it, Bea, lost it completely.'

"The tale of my birth in the willow tree, and the years of my growth to maturity, unfolded. *No doubt, you're cracked, but how blissful to think someone cares, even if you are loopy*, I thought.

"Still shaken at the end of His story I heard the words, 'Bea, perhaps now is the season for you to learn the meaning of service.' From that hour, He's been my number-two hero.

"Sammie is in line to be my number-three hero. He taught me how to find food near the borders of the pond. My grubbings were acceptable until the rains fell at summer's end. The rigors of losing my delicacies for a season strengthened me. After a time, he and I became Syntee's messengers."

"Bea, your story sounds like one of the fabutales Mom used to read to me."

"Maybe so. Such stories can reflect wishes, dreams, or happenings in our life. Not every character in a fabutale lives hap-

33

pily ever after, just the main ones. I'm the main one in my story."

"Yes you are, you little princess," Jal agreed.

"More about fabutales later, in former times called fairy tales. By the way, Jal, my full name is Beatrice Caroline."

"I'm not likely to forget such a pretty name, though I like Bea; it fits you. My name is Joulh, but Mom didn't want any confusion between my Uncle Joulh and me. So, Jal it is."

"And you, Sammie, how did you meet Syntee? And your name, Sammie, what is your other name?"

"Here is the story of Samuel Barrington Coburne to answer your questions. Years ago, Jal, my wife, Neda, and I—"

"A wife, Sammie!"

"Wait a minute, I'll explain. Yes, a wife, a still dearly loved wife. We joyed in our wonderland, our days sailing on the water; our evenings in our home of reeds and rushes; the streams and lakes...

"To go on...one summer we planned a holiday for the two of us. It seems but yesterday, even though the years have mounted up. We wanted to go further south and spent hours discussing the places to visit. One late autumn day, a bit after sunrise, we set off. I can still see the morning sun tipping her wings with a gilt of gold. We were flying low directly over an open field. Without warning, there came a loud noise and a whirring sound. Neda cried out. Alarmed, I swerved in flight and my heart almost failed; her left wing was drooping.

"She managed to fly into a grove of trees, where I had to admit to myself that her wound was serious. My anguish was so shattering I couldn't move; I lay at her side, mute and lifeless. She leaned her head on my shoulder and said, 'Sammie, please listen to me. You must be brave. I am going on alone; we both know it has to be. It's only for a little while. I'll wait for you in the place we have often talked about—the Beautiful Land. Let this be your comfort until we're together again.

"'Please, Sammie, pay attention to what I'm telling you. Fill your days with useful tasks while you wait to join me. Put your grief aside, my dear one. When next we meet, I expect you to be my same gallant Sammie. Don't you dare show up as some broken, helpless being I won't even recognize. I love you and will be waiting for you.' And then she left me.

"Unaware of the passing hours, I held her in my arms. As the dawn approached I glimpsed a nearby stream of swift-running water. I gave her body to the stream and watched while she was carried from my sight. In late morning, I started walking to an adjoining village. Neda's words rang in my head and gave me the strength to persevere.

"In the late afternoon, I crept under the branches of the willow tree. I lay for hours, so numb with grief I could only whimper. Then I felt something like a soft caressing hand touch my face. And a soothing whisper came: 'Sammie, Sammie, your sorrow indeed is great.'

"Dazed, I got up and looked over the place where I lay. Finding nothing, I slumped back down.

"The whisper came again, 'Sammie, Sammie, listen to me!'

"Like you, Jal, I walked, or more likely crawled, about the tree searching for someone. I heard the words, 'You will stay by me until your grief has spent its strong force. Here, you are to make your home and find useful tasks to do.'

"And that, Jal, is how I met Syntee. In the afternoon, Bea came home from a scouting jaunt to a permanent guest. She was in a good mood after successfully uncovering a treasure trove of her edibles. 'I'll accept you,' she said, 'but you must steer clear of my necessaries.' I acceded readily to her whim.

"To sum up, my strength grew as my grief tapered off in the succeeding days. The darkness, which had engulfed me when I lost my Neda, began to lighten. Bea and I were diligent students, and within the year, Syntee instated us as messengers.

"Like Bea, it seems long years ago. Her home sits high in the willow tree; she dubbed it the penthouse. Syntee assigned the pond to me."

"The pond, Sammie? Was that the pool I saw you in this morning? You were staring at the tree."

"The very one, Jal. It was the signal for mission orders. That's why I stared.

"To finish my story...

"When the time comes to rejoin my Neda, she will find a heroic confidant, one devoted to her. The hope of our reunion is ever in my heart."

Jal pondered Sammie's story with awe. No words came to him. He considered his earlier thoughts. *Oh, that I could be a swan, I would then be free from all my troubles.*

"No questions, Sammie. Thank you."

"And you, Jal," he said, "we're familiar with your story. Syntee has informed us. We'll tell you how before our trek ends."

As they walked, Jal reached out and touched Sammie affectionately. *I want to learn to have courage and be strong like Sammie,* he said to himself.

The path began to ascend in winding curves beside the stream. In the silence, Jal became conscious of the sunlight flickering in the treetops and the rustlings in the underbrush. The undertones of the burbling stream deepened to a clear timbre. On the other side of the stream, a golden shadow moved through the grasses. Astounded, he watched it disappear and blurted out, "Did you see a shadow?" He waved his hand toward the grasses.

"Yes," Bea said airily, "Eli is passing by. He's a chief messenger of Syntee. We work with him now and again."

"But...who is Eli? How can a shadow be golden?"

"You'll know soon enough. We'll stay the night with him tomorrow." She changed the subject. "Time for lunch. Let's refresh ourselves a spell by the stream."

Sammie had discreetly moved away during their conversation. He rejoined them, carrying two paper bags. He handed one to Jal containing vegetable soup, a thick slice of grainy bread, an apple, and a pack of mixed nuts. "Extra soup, since we ate no breakfast."

"Thank you, Sammie. When I left my room...seems like a hundred years ago, I stuck a sandwich in my backpack. Sometime during the night I ate it. Quelled my hunger pangs while I moaned."

"Quell again," Bea said while sipping sipped nectar from a cup. Sammie ate greens and grains and watched their by-play.

"Where did you get the luscious food?" Jal asked as they moved to sit on a rock by the stream.

"Syntee said that your needs would be met on this journey. You will know in good time. Wait the unveiling," Bea replied.

Jal was content to listen to the stream's melodic trilling. *The stream has a voyage, and we have a journey,* he said to himself while viewing his wavering face in the moving waters.

5

Back on the pathway, Jal's thoughts reverted to Eli. From time to time, he scanned the grasses, hoping to catch another glimpse of the mutable shadow. The path narrowed as it led uphill, and he walked by the side of Sammie. The air became chilly in the higher elevation, and Jal zipped up his jacket and asked, "Why is it so cold here, Sammie?"

"Arctic chill?" Sammie replied. "I put a liner in your pocket earlier, the very item to keep you warm."

Jal added the liner to his jacket while gazing in disbelief at the odd sight in front of him. A fence of ice, three or four feet high, surrounded a massive dome-like space. A net of frozen droplets spilled from the fence in a spectrum of colors. Blocks of ice sitting on sheets of an ice-covered substance coasted in their direction. Loud discordant sounds came from them like growls. Taken aback, Jal gaped at them. Pale gray eyes glinted from atop the block bodies as if they were looking through glass. Rendered speechless, Jal stood gaping at Bea and Sammie and spluttered out, "That…that…what is that?"

"That?" Sammie said. "That is the land of the Frozen Ones. Let's hustle, Jal. The Frozen Ones have a habit of waylaying idlers here. Lots of entries but no exits. Only one little fellow found a way out. We'll tell you about him later."

A group of the ice blocks came to the fence and beckoned to Jal while Sammie was speaking. He held steadily to Sammie and gasped out, "Stupendous, this place is! Don't you think so Sammie?"

"The beauty can't be denied; their architectural talent is without equal, but beings such as you and I wouldn't be comfortable in their city."

"True, Sammie," Bea said, folding her wings flat to her body. "Brrr...brrr, just thinking about it makes me shiver."

Jal refrained from speaking until the frozen land was behind them. The mild warmth permeated the atmosphere as before. He removed the jacket liner and replaced it in his pocket. "Those blocks of ice, Sammie? Off the wall, literally. Did you understand what they said?"

"Let me get my breath, and I'll tell you the story. Yes, I catch a few words of their speech, it's a variation of English. It was their customary invitation. They were luring us in. And by the way, they are known as the Kulkuks to the outside world," Sammie broke off a minute, as if in thought.

"Do go on, Sammie," Jal said.

"Long years before you or I were born, they were citizens of a nation advanced in the physical sciences. The nation fostered their specialties and shared all discoveries with a grateful world—for example, valuable innovations in medicine. At first, their scientific experts acted in an advisory capacity to governing councils. As time went by, they began to move directly into administrative posts of government. They increased their authority by giving generous service in a self-effacing manner. Then it mushroomed as the nation's influence grew.

"Threats of imprisonment reduced the public's opposition to their policies. Resistance groups sprouted up and went underground. Over a span of years they defeated the scientists by legal means.

"The scientists, however, refused to accept their loss. In a defiant lecture to the nation, they said, 'You repudiate our rule even though you benefit from the prosperity we provide to the country. We've earned the right to govern. Since you prefer a less-progressive way of life, we will create a state of our own. To our loyal supporters, we extend an invitation to help us in the building of our glorious republic.' They titled themselves the Savants and founded a site in an adjacent country with few inhabitants.

"The local residents living on the fringes of the Savants' property declined to be part of the new enterprise, but a fair

41

number of the world's inhabitants joined them. The scientists governed with more subtle methods and developed their city gradually. It was a city of great beauty, and they named it, Tergadare. The Savants retained power by using highly developed electronic devices to monitor the citizens. Social and physical scientists from every nation gathered to study their techniques. Plans to build a country went by the wayside; they seemed content to focus on Tergadare."

"I would like to see that city, Sammie. Do you think we could visit sometime?"

"Alas, Jal, the city is now the Frozen Land, beautiful but forbidding. Visitors are neither welcomed nor permitted. They invite passersby to enter on a permanent basis. Once in, no out.

"To digress a minute, the nations have applied the Savants' policies in a number of ways, some to better life for their citizens and others to wield power.

"The World Confederation has been through tough periods with these rogue nations. Several countries developed despotic regimes that weakened the WC's ability to govern. Negotiations brought two penitents back into the fold, but about ten countries pulled out of the confederation.

"Most likely, the current WC concerns are summarized in your civic lessons. We'll refer to its evolution at another time. These bits of information might be useful when you're back into your coursework. For now though, let's finish our Kulkuk story."

"I never read anything about the Kulkuks in my civics or history, Sammie. I wonder why. Not even in Civil Manners and Behavior, a prep course for the IGM."

"I have no idea, Jal. Perhaps in a later course you will. I do know the censors of the WC finely sift the international curriculum. And tell me, what is the IGM?"

"It's the Institute of Government Management where governing principles are taught. Each year HQ selects twelve students from the four districts. I was on the list to enter the academy this year."

"Elite, no less, Bea, or a smart cookie. What do you say?"

"I say he's a prize-winning boy, dutiful in his studies, Sammie."

"Yes, I do well in my classwork. So that's that. Anyhow, proceed, Sammie."

"The populace grew in knowledge, and the expertise of the Savants—I'm referring to the leaders—became less relevant. They seemed at a loss...until hitting on a campaign to criticize the public. Trust went by the wayside, and the city's life was at a stalemate.

The Savants devised experimental weapons to restrain the inhabitants. Regulations were ineffective to control the situation, the president's aide proclaimed. The leaders conveniently ignored their culpability in creating the situation. Not long after, a catastrophe happened; to the outside world, it came as no shock.

"The neighboring residents got up one morning and remarked on the city's eerie appearance. A closer inspection disclosed a globe-like dome of opaque ice encircling the city. In a flash, the incident was front-page news. Repeated attempts failed to break through the icy shield. The rescuers ultimately figured out that removal from the inside was the only solution.

"You can imagine the world's curiosity —the media had a field day for weeks. In time, the icy globe cleared to a semi-transparent shield and formed droplets. What a sensation, a cause célèbre!"

"Wow, Sammie, some sight, I betcha. I never read their annals. Why not?"

"As I mentioned before, Jal, the WC censors are pretty busy in the history field, but the story is well known in this country.

"Eventually, the Savants issued a communiquè. In no way did they want to leave their city or comfortable icy homes. 'In fact, an invite stands to join us,' the leaders said. Soon after, all outside communication ended. Most seem to be happy with their way of life, as the one who escaped tells us. More about him later. The Savants gave up their governing ambitions; their appetite for ruling was done in. We learned they resigned their positions, but in spite of everything, they persist in their dotty scientific experiments. I guess theirs is one way to circumvent the outer world's interference, although a dreadful one."

6

The path wound round a stand of trees with brilliant red leaves, and the topic of the frozen land sputtered out. Jal climbed upward with the gurgling stream on his right and reflected on the strange beings that were so outside his experience. *Weird, a lot to ponder!* The lengthening shadows on the ground indicated the approach of evening.

Sammie broke into his thoughts. "We'll reach the guesthouse by sunset."

"Another question, Sammie. Why couldn't I see the stream while we were passing the Kulkuks' land? We were still on the path."

"It happened this way, Jal. The Kulkuks wanted control of the resources on their land and any others they could filch. They diverted the running streams for their exclusive use. Our stream lies outside their boundaries. It's off limits even though they applied their major engineering skills to the harnessing of the water. Once the attempt to take possession failed, the architects altered their designs to place Tergadare on the periphery of the stream.

"'Perhaps when the population increases another attempt will bring us what we most want,' they fumed to one another. And thus, they pacified their ambitions for the interim.

"Syntee, though, undermined their goal. He channeled the stream to prevent any future conflicts.

"On the morning when the Kulkuks were making merry in honor of their city's completion, the long-established boundaries of the stream disappeared. It remains a riddle to them. As a rebuke to the Kulkuks, the water they so desired has been denied their grasp.

"The stream isn't an exclusive right of any particular group. The property belongs to our country, and everyone who walks our way shares in the beauty. Any Kulkuk who looks on the stream has an open invitation to join our country. The path we travel is an ancient and unchanging way."

"Thank you, Sammie. Incredible! Everything is; there's so much to think about I'm going to adjourn thinking for a while. I put off my studies sometimes when Mom went shopping."

"I'm sure your mom was aware of your need for a break, Jal. And a wanted break is waiting for us in a few minutes," Sammie said.

The chatter of the birds and the rustlings of the creatures in the woods subsided as nightfall approached. The shadows had deepened to a charcoal-gray.

"Here we are, Jal," Bea said.

"Where?" He strained to pick out a building in the dimness.

"There. Forest colored," she said and flew into the dusk.

A pinpoint of light gleamed from the window of a cedar-shingled building set among the trees. One broad stone step led up to a porch running its length.

Sammie opened the door and motioned for Jal to step inside. He went in and checked out the neat room, which was fitted with two beds and an open shelved cabinet. Boxed containers of food were on a table with glasses, a few utensils, and a yellow bowl containing a variety of fruits. Sammie picked up a note and read aloud, "Milk in spring in rear of house. Welcome to your new country, Jal." Going out, he immediately brought back two pitchers filled with a fruit drink and milk.

On each bed lay nightclothes and clean clothes for the next day. Under one of the beds, a pair of new ankle-high shoes caught Jal's attention. He went closer and inspected them. "Are these boots for me, Sammie?"

"The boots are yours, Jal," he replied. "You need sturdy footwear for our day-long hikes. Leave the old ones for cleaning and any needed repairs. A package containing renewed shoes will be at your door within the month. We tend to stretch the wear of our togs in this country."

Jal carefully slid his stockinged feet into the boots. "My feet did get tired, Sammie, but I didn't want to say anything.

I'm glad to get these. They feel good, just the right size. Who knew I needed shoes?"

"Later, Jal; let's wash up and eat, I'm starving. But first... look—my own bedroom!" Bea said. A door stenciled in a flower and leaf design opened in a miniature cabinet and revealed a bedroom with a fan-shaped window framed by red and white floral curtains. "No view from the window, but I wanted one anyway." She motioned to a ceramic basin. "My bath. Isn't it pretty?"

"Positively, Bea. But I need a magnifying glass to see it up close."

"Jal Valhyn, if my basin was bigger, I'd soak your head in it," she said testily. "You waggish thing."

"Cut. Abridge your act. Grab your trunks, soap and towel. And a robe, too." Sammie opened a door near his bed and entered a bathroom with towels, soap, and toothbrushes.

"Neat Sammie," Jal said, gathering up the items. "I'll try out my new shoes by walking to the stream in them."

"Location pinpointed. Meet you there, guys," Bea said." My pink frilled togs will get a water workout."

Sammie and Jal exited the cabin and minutes later were basking in a pool of surprisingly warm water.

"Luxuriant, the gift of the stream!" Bea exclaimed.

"I know what luxuriant means. It means having Mom, Dad, and Uncle Joulh with me. Do you think I'll have a long wait, Sammie?"

"Think about what Syntee said, Jal. Consider His words. Your mom and dad are getting updates on our travels and destination; they may join you sooner than you think."

"I'll chuck the thoughts and focus on dinner. I'm hungry, Sammie, and so tired; I bet I could sleep a week."

"This water feels so good, doesn't it, Bea? My bath was never like this."

"Yes, to everything you've said, except the last. I've no idea how your bath was. Let's go eat. Meet you at the cabin." Bea whizzed into the air.

When Sammie and Jal went in, she was daintily sipping her nectar. "I waited for you guys. I only drank a little, and I apologize."

"You're excused this once. Isn't she, Jal?" chided Sammie. "Practice your manners and wait for us next time."

"Okay, I will. Here, I'll help to put your food out. I'll get Jal's glass."

"No, a definite no. You sit right there and sip your nectar. I don't want you picking up a vessel of any kind. Too heavy for you to carry."

"Okay, thank you." She attended to her sipping.

"Bea has a big appetite for such a little creature," Sammie said to Jal.

"I'm beginning to decode that. Doesn't take much translating."

"You two quit talking about me. I'm in the room," Bea said crossly.

Sammie and Jal winched up their eyebrows and looked at one another. "Chow your grubbings," Sammie said. "Best thing to do, Jal. "

A salad, barley soup, and grain bread with a fruit juice and milk satisfied Jal's hunger. Bea sipped her nectar with gusto.

"You do seem to relish your food," Jal said.

"You're the whiz kid on the enjoyment of food, the way you've been chomping," Bea retorted. They beamed at each other.

"Most appetizing," Sammie averred.

"I'd still like to learn who brought the food here. I'm likely to be a pest, Sammie and Bea, until I do. Dad says, 'You're a relentless interrogator, Jal.'"

"When you're home in your new digs, you can refurbish your interrogation skills," Bea said cheerfully. "Syntee has various messengers and helpers on the routes we travel. We can't tell you the specific ones of our bounty, but curiosity requires answers. And you will get yours. Perseverance is the word."

Seated on the step of the cabin after dinner cleanup, they talked over the day's journey.

"I admit I can't make it out. 'No head or tails,' as my Uncle Joulh says. When I tell Mom and Dad the Kulkuk story, they'll say, 'Your imagination is running on overdrive, Jal.' I did invent stories sometimes but a whopper, never. About the Kulkuk who escaped the frozen city—please tell me his quandary tomorrow, Sammie. I'm too tired to listen tonight."

"Remind me in the morning, and the quandary it shall be."

The twilight ebbed away, marking the end of the day. Fireflies flickered against the backdrop of the dusky night. Overhead, the moon appeared as a bright crescent in the heavens. The stars multiplied in the deepening darkness. "A presentation just for us," remarked Bea.

"A memorable debut for me," Jal said. "Much better than the musical arcade."

They entered the cabin, ready for a good night's sleep. Bea grazed Jal's face with a delicate wing. "Night to a poetic sprite." She disappeared into her bedroom, humming a tune.

Sammie and Jal fell into bed, weary after the long, eventful day. Jal collapsed with a grateful sigh and pulled the sweet-smelling sheet up to his chin. He glanced at Sammie, who was already sleeping. His gaze rested on the etchings of Bea's bedroom door. *What a pleasant day—the tiring walk, my shoes, and the stars; things to store in my memory bundle.* He reviewed the happenings from his meeting Syntee to his arrival at the guesthouse. *Wait 'til I tell Mom! Don't exaggerate, Jal, that's what she'll say.* With these thoughts, he fell into an undisturbed sleep without the recurrent unsettling dream. The assurance of safety, instilled in the course of the day's journey, imparted tranquil rest.

Second Day
7

He awoke to the low voices of Sammie and Bea, who were setting out the morning's breakfast. Opening one eye, he looked at them through his lashes. He then tightly closed both eyes and shook his head from side to side, as if to make certain Bea and Sammie weren't figments of his imagination. He said in a shaky voice, "Sammie, Bea, good morning."

Bea set her nectar in place and replied, "Yes, we're real—and here in this cabin, Jal. No doubt from this end. Good morning to you. Be a darling boy and come to breakfast. Time to get ready for our day's journey. We leave at sunrise."

Jal got up, showered, put on his robe, and came to the table. Sammie placed a glass of milk, bread, and a bowl of grain with fruit in front of him. He touched and then tasted the unknown cereal and decided it was luscious. He ate and asked for more.

Sammie packed their lunch and wrote a note while Jal dressed in his clean clothes and put his boots on. He folded his worn ones and placed them on the bed. He swept the floor and helped Bea wash the few breakfast dishes. *Now who gets the note?* he thought, and then said, "Sammie, don't forget to write a thank you for my boots."

"Already done, and off we go."

On their exit, Sammie pinned the message to the door. The morning sun gilded the treetops as they reached the shaded path. *Later, I'll ask about the note,* Jal said to himself. He became conscious of the shape of the tree leaves and the color of the wildflowers. He touched the trees, sometimes reaching out to feel the variance in their bark. *Funny, each is different and the leaves too. Maybe Syntee meant I would learn these things.* The thought cheered him. The rustlings of the wood creatures beginning their day interrupted his thoughts. Round, dark eyes peered at him from the underbrush.

"Sammie, do animals live on Grandfather Moutyn's property?"

"Of course, Jal," Sammie replied. "Abundant animals, big and little, live on the farms. The forested woodlands are chockfull of wild creatures. In this country, Jal, there's enough room for every type of creature to have a spacious home.

"Today, we'll pass by the Dazidazlers. We keep our distance from them, as they like to tease passersby. Their appearance is so farfetched onlookers are easily frightened. Their playful tricks are notorious; consequently, it's important to stay on the path."

"Who are the Dazidazlers?" Jal queried.

"Theirs is an old story. Would you like to tell him, Bea?"

"No, you carry on, Sammie."

"Okay," he agreed. "But first, the story of the little fellow, Cecil, who escaped or rather, ran away from home."

"Please. You didn't forget, Sammie?"

"No, I'm forever ready to tell his story. A fine fellow is Cecil. Eli found him on the pathway, ill and terribly weak, when he was fourteen years of age. He was lying in a puddle of water. You can guess what happened. Cecil's lack of knowledge of drastic temperature changes almost did him in. Obviously, outside...Through Eli's timely rescue, and the aid of Ben, a scientist who lives on the farm, he revived.

"Ben carefully monitored the thawing process for several months. 'I confess to being confounded by the short, talkative, and self-assured adolescent who leaked out from the ice,' he says, when telling the story.

"Cecil refused the offer to send him home. 'I want to stay right here and be a scientist like Ben. I've dreamed about the outside world for a long time, and it's more than I imagined it to be. At night, in my bed, I gazed up at the stars and fantasized about escaping. I often stayed awake until dawn. The sky was murky because the dome was between us. I marveled at the multitude of stars even though they approximated old Tom who drank malt whiskey. He lived next door and came home at night teetering from side to side.

"'My desire to see the stars clearly strengthened with each passing year. The dome that screened my home was a piddling thing compared to the vastness of the sky. The tinseled globules of the dome are no equal to its brilliance,' he told us.

"'I looked up and saw the stars. I looked down and saw the path; I looked out and saw the passersby, and I wanted to know where the path was taking them. I'm an orphan anyway. No one will miss me. I guess I have to get used to aging in this country. Living under the frozen shield conferred perpetual youth. Everyone remained whatever age he or she was at the time of the cataclysm. Aging can't be too bad. I long since got tired of being fourteen years old. Never-ending years.'

"And so, Jal, Cecil grew up and became a nutritional scientist, working with Ben and Porter. Because the ice compressed his body, he remains short in stature, somewhat like the custom of compressing feet hundreds of years ago, he says. Your introduction to him is in order, possibly tonight."

"Sammie, that's some story, but tell me how Cecil escaped from the dome. What did you say the scientist's name was?"

"Ben is his name," Bea cut in. "He's tall and slim, and Cecil is short and blocky. They're the best of friends. Ben's fiancée is a teacher at the nutritional facility, but we haven't met her yet. Their marriage is to take place at the first communal gathering in January. We'll meet her then. I'm getting my outfit ready, a snazzy one."

"Sorry, Sammie, for disrupting your story."

"I'm talking loads on this trip without your usual interjections. You're excused.

"To answer your question, Jal, about Cecil's getaway," Sammie continued, "I forgot to mention how he bolted. Years went into planning before he figured out a scheme of escape. In order for the Kulkuks to survive, they devised a system to maintain a consistent temperature below freezing. Their bodies get somewhat slushy on exertion, so every day they replenish the ice in a special chamber. For hygienic reasons, their bodily sediments are flushed through a drain to the outside. On a day when Cecil had charge of the task, he put a mask on and wriggled inside the drain.

"'It was horribly uncomfortable, coming through that drain,' he told us with a grimace."

Bea added. "Sort of like me coming out of that contraption called a cocoon."

"I imagine it was Bea," Sammie replied. "No, mean feat, that! Anyway...elated at reaching the outside, Cecil made it to the path by crawling an inch at a time. That's where Eli came in."

"You tell good stories, Sammie. I can hardly wait to meet Cecil and Ben. Let's walk a while before the Dazidazler story. Let me think on Cecil and his escape. A daffy country he lived in."

"Well spoken, Jal, and our route is decidedly pleasing for the next half hour, so let's tune in to the scenery."

They made a U-turn on the pathway into a more lush setting as Sammie spoke. Low, flowering shrubs in mixed colors flourished on each side of the path.

"This place reminds me of the botanical garden we used to visit on Sunday afternoon," Jal said.

"You can go to botanical gardens here if you wish. There are lots of them in this country," Bea said. "Would you like to sit by the stream awhile and absorb the décor?"

And so, in the soft morning sun amid the gurgles of the stream, they savored Callie's pastries. "We picnicked by a waterfall when Mom and Dad were home on leave," Jal said in a pensive tone.

"Thank you, Bea and Sammie. I'm through for now and ready to go. Your story—I want to hear the story of the Dazidazlers."

"Long years ago," Sammie began once they were on the path, "the Dazidazlers lived in a Southern country rather like yours. Splendid rivers and cities surrounded their home in a beautiful valley. Why they became fearful, we don't know. But a phobia based on outsider groups developed and rapidly spread among the residents. They lived in terror that some group would take their valley from them.

"Perhaps a multiplicity of newcomers moved into the area. Whatever the reason, they set out to discover ways to protect their territory. The years went by, they grew more fearful, and their weapons more fearsome. They worked day and night to achieve their goal of security. Joy in everyday life ceased, and the beauty of their valley began to decay. Oddly enough, few seemed to take note or care.

"Then, a dreadful accident happened. Massive firestorms erupted and lasted for months. The present beings materialized when the inferno ended. Not one has come outside yet to tell the story, unlike Cecil.

"Eli makes a point of traveling this way at monthly intervals. He never fails to get his man or woman, so we hazard a guess, Bea and I. One day we'll meet a Dazidazler when we are either coming or going on an assignment.

"Enough speculating; the accident took place about the time the Kulkuks appeared on the scene. It was a period of historic peace. The why or how is unknown. No written records exist. When we question Syntee, He says, 'Expand your capacity for analysis and judgment. In time you will understand.' Expansion is extra slow in reaching us! We're to give the place a go-by. Eli can deal with them. Whatever the reason, they don't tease him.

"The one time we disobeyed, Syntee—what a harrying experience; a lesson dearly bought. Safety is crucial to our missions, meaning total obedience to Syntee's instructions."

Red clouds appeared in the distance. Gigantic, blazing orbs blanketed the landscape. From translucent buildings of fire, flames jetted into the sky then tapered off and coursed along the ground.

"Bears a resemblance to a conflagration," Sammie commented, "but it isn't. Ever burning but strictly pyrotechnic, a staged drama to impress passersby."

Jal gaped at the spectacular scene while asking, "What is conflagration, Sammie?"

"Conflagration is destructive fire that consumes everything, but no consuming here," Sammie explained.

Inside a wall of fire, slender reeds of flame raced toward the path but collapsed before reaching it.

Curious, I feel no heat, Jal thought.

"Teasing us," Bea said. "The Dazidazlers mimic the shooting blazes of the buildings. You'd think they'd try an alternate act occasionally. Let's hurry on. We can eat our lunch and talk about them if you wish."

To Jal's relief, they were soon past. The tree-shaded path in vivid greens was a comforting sight. The sunlit spangles under their feet appeared to beckon them onward. The stream seemed to be singing an extra-joyous tune.

8

The Dazidazlers faded into the background of Jal's thoughts as the image of the golden shadow reappeared. The swaying of the grasses reminded him they were to spend the night with Eli.

"Lunch time with a pleasing site," Sammie said, breaking into Jal's thoughts. "Here, we can sit on this rock big enough for two and a smidgeon of another."

Bea said huffily, "You aren't talking to me, are you, Sammie?"

"Why ever would I refer to you as a smidgeon, Bea? Let's eat, my lady."

The rock shaped like a bench diverted Bea's thoughts, and the stream's offering of a musicale relieved her pique.

"This nectar is an especiale' of Ben's, an irk soother," she said.

"We'll thank Ben for his soothsaying skills on your behalf," Sammie replied.

Jal's paper bag contained a sandwich of cheese and tomato on brown bread, an apple, and a chocolate drink. Sammie and Bea had their grains and nectar.

"The food is so good," Jal said. "The walking makes me extra hungry too."

"It does indeed," Sammie said.

"Jal, do you have any questions about the Dazidazlers?" Bea inquired.

"I didn't feel any heat. Why was that?"

"Whatever caused the firestorm had some kind of a scientific basis dealing with cold instead of heat. I can't explain further. The science of it is beyond Sammie and me. Better ask Grandfather Moutyn. He knows a ton of things."

"I guess other questions can be boxed. It's so overwhelming, like the dream where I'm searching for my mom and dad. I can't get rid of the gummy thing. It has taken up lodgings. Once I cried so loud, Uncle Joulh woke up. He held me until I fell asleep again. No dreams came last night, maybe they got unstuck."

"I can't hold you if you have a bad dream, but I can soothe you with a song." Bea said. "No need of concern for the frightful Dazidazlers; they love their fiery home. Moreover, their lofty mathematicians are capable of reversing the effects of the firestorm. They prefer their present way of life, and that's true of the other offbeat groups. The path we travel remains an open invitation; our country encourages their citizenship.

"Let's talk of the pleasant prospect ahead of us today—a subject most agreeable to me." Bea patted Jal's head. "We'll be with Eli and Molly this evening. I've a stack of their stories. Would you like to hear one or two?"

Sammie, sitting calmly, eating his food, nodded. "She is loaded up on odds and ends at that, Jal. So it's best to let her tell you."

A picture of the golden shadow leapt to Jal's mind. "Yes, I would," he said. "Who are Eli and Molly? You didn't answer me when I asked you before. "

"The story will be told in good time," she replied breezily to his reproachful tone.

Sammie broke in, "Wait a minute, Bea. A good time to go. We've had a late lunch; we'd better get on. Molly expects our arrival before dinner."

On the path, Bea took up her story where she had left off. "I did mention Eli is one of Syntee's chief messengers, Jal. His land holdings are extensive, with masses of residents living and working on the farm. Molly is Eli's household manager, and you will meet Callie, Porter, and Montague. The newest addition to the family is Louisa Victoria. She prefers Missy, the name given to her by her mother.

"Sammie and I visit so often, Molly set aside bedrooms for us. We attend their three yearly gatherings whenever we can. I must say, everyone loves get-togethers and celebrations. One could stay on the go from one to the other for the entire year.

"Eli's home is a hospitality center for all and sundry; for some, it's the end of the journey, and for others it's a wayside rest stop. Syntee decides the most suitable place for each new immigrant, as he did with you.

"In this country, Jal, we strive to live a simple life, but nonetheless, one that is comfortable. A plain lifestyle doesn't mean a lack of beauty; we consider beauty an essential. The delectable foods and the clothes you're wearing attest to the fact. You'll gain a greater awareness of what I'm saying when you meet Eli's family circle."

"A lot to take in, Bea. I'm dizzy from it all," Jal said. "Tell me, though, while I'm gyrating, why is Eli on the other side of the stream instead of with us?"

Sammie replied to his question after exchanging glances with Bea. "In addition to his special duties, Eli serves as a protector. He's up to date on our movements but busy with various matters, and it's best we walk alone. I'll tell you later how Eli gets his news. You'll learn to trust him in next to no time. Wait and see.

"Multitudes of foodstuffs grow on the farm; in addition, fruit orchards, vineyards, and a dairy are on the premises. A research facility, located on the grounds, employs a number of nutritional scientists. Cecil, the wee fellow we spoke of, is one of them. He looks ordinary but is a bit paler and shorter than most. We can thank him for the delectable qualities of the foods we're eating. Since the mystery of our rations has been solved, more of Eli's story later."

"Okay, Sammie, no problem. The secret of the food is identified, but the subject of Eli is daunting and requires a slow go."

The path led upward, the trees grew denser, and wildflowers carpeted the ground. Eyes in furry bodies peeked out from the undergrowth. They scampered away into the underbrush when Jal caught sight of them. The birds, busy with their tasks, chattered to one another in their varied ways.

"The birds are at their posts," Bea said. "They work, just as we do."

"I've never thought about the birds working. Do the animals work too, Bea?"

"Yes, they do."

"Then, I guess my work was my studies. Now, my work must be this traveling. Right, Bea?"

"Right you are. Learning while traveling. Impromptu drills and other training yet to come."

"Is language a part of the training, Bea?"

"The study of language is important and your assignments will include it. Understanding speech patterns is an asset in this country because the residents are from every section of the world."

"It's Dad, Bea; I've been studying language for three years now. 'An addition to your classical education, Jal,' he said. 'Why not a subtraction, Dad.' I said. 'Get to your class Jal, or I'll be multiplying penalties for you,' he said."

"You listen to your dad, Jal. Lots of things we don't understand right away, but in time we do."

"Do you think so, Sammie?"

"Sorted and approved. We garner gems from unlikely sources, even language studies. Consider the slang terms we're using from two hundred years ago." Sammie replied.

The way became less steep as they rounded a sharp curve. They walked the path in silence while Jal meditated on Bea and Sammie's remarks.

9

The sun was low on the horizon as they mounted the crest of the hill. Jal came to a standstill, enthralled by the setting that lay before him. A picturesque green valley ringed with rolling hills stretched far into the distance. Stone buildings dotted the landscape and gave an ageless patina to the scene.

"This is Eli's home," Sammie said. "A place of unequaled beauty."

A large white house sat on a grassy plateau with a verandah of stone columns on three sides of its square shape. The lawn sloped downward and drew the eyes to a mega-sized willow tree on the bank of the stream.

Jal's thoughts returned to the night he slept under the willow tree. *Looks like Syntee's tree, a tree of rescue.*

They entered a graveled walkway bounded by yellow flowering cassia trees, edged by flowers in pale blue shading to darker blues and purple. "What a pretty place!" Jal exclaimed.

"Yes," Bea said merrily. "This house is fit for a king."

Jal, curious, began to speak; but just then, someone appeared in the doorway dressed in white with a blue apron covering the front of her dress. Pale flaxen hair framed a warm, gentle face with bright brown eyes smiling at them.

"Molly!" Bea exclaimed. "Here we are, Molly, right on time."

"My precious ones, come in. A break for pampering is on order. You must be hungry after the climb you've had today. We'll soon have dinner ready."

She took Jal's hands in hers, "You are expected, my dear. Please, accept our hospitality." Molly kept Jal's hand in hers as they entered the hallway.

A broad stairway, carpeted in red, led to the upstairs. *Grand,* Jal thought as he appraised the room. Off to the right, someone in the kitchen walked from the sink to a large table.

"Callie," Molly said. "They're here at long last. Bea and Sammie, with our guest."

"Excuse me, be in directly. I'm taking the bread out of the oven."

Presently, she came out dressed in yellow with orange stripes. A white apron and a yellow scarf completed her ensemble. "Our intrepid travelers. My, what a handsome fellow you are, Jal. It's a pleasure to have you in our home." Her citrine-colored eyes, set in a triangular face, looked into his for a long moment; satisfied with the result, she took his hand and put it to her lips. *Just like a calico cat, but a pretty one*, Jal thought approvingly.

"We'll talk later; I want to tend to your special treat," she said.

Molly led them upstairs to their rooms. Each had a bedroom, including a bath. Bea said, "I know where mine is; I've slept here enough."

"Have a moment's respite. Clean clothes are in your closets, and something new for one little girl. Dinner will be early today—right away, in fact. Yell if you need anything; I'll be downstairs with Callie. Incidentally, Porter and Montague are due any minute, and Eli expects to join us."

Bea withdrew to her bedroom after an imperative, "Hurry up, you guys, I'm hungry."

Jal and Sammie grinned at one another and went to their rooms. After showering and changing clothes, they came out to find Bea staring at herself in a hallway mirror. "My new pink dress, isn't it lovely? And this matching hat. I'll wear it to Ben's wedding. A 1940's creation."

Sammie glanced at Jal. "Indeed, your dress is lovely. The hat is chic, and that veil is so outré," they intoned in an out-of-sync harmony.

"Of course, I'll leave it in the closet after dinner and do a pick up on our way home. Syntee must have a peek. I like new dresses, especially in pink. You two quit grinning. Your odious acts are outrageous. I'll put the hat in my room, wait a blink."

They descended the stairs to the sound of animated voices in the dining room. An energetic male voice intermingled in the conversational chorus.

He swiveled around to greet them. "Hey partners, you're here! A new dress, eh, Bea? A pretty girl in a pretty dress."

"And who is this young lad? I'm Porter, by the way," he said in a jovial voice, beaming at Jal. Dressed in blue overalls with a striped hat of the same blue color, he was quite pudgy with a genial face and merry green eyes.

His manner was so affable that Jal walked up to him and said, "I'm Jal, Porter," and shook his hand.

A banging and clattering outside the entrance to the kitchen interrupted them. The door opened, and the most outlandish being Jal had ever seen walked in.

Molly spoke. "Monty, dinner is ready. Did you meet Eli on your way in?"

"Yes, he'll be here in five minutes or so." Unmoving, Jal studied the quaint being dressed in top hat and tails. with a blunderbuss under his arm. Standing the object upright in a cupboard, he saluted Bea and Sammie effusively. He shook Jal's hand and went out, saying, "I'll only be a sec."

"That's Montague?" Jal asked in a quizzical tone.

"Yes, call him Monty," Molly said. 'I'm more a Monty than a Montague,' he says. Here—would you mind helping, please?" She handed him a platter of biscuits. Jal took a few steps and placed the dish on the long dinner table. He opened his mouth to speak to Molly and found himself unable to utter a word.

A golden giant stood in the dining room doorway observing him. The giant stepped to the large chair at the head of the table and sat down. "Welcome, Jal, to our home. I am Eli."

The vivid figure of a golden shadow slipping through the grasses resurfaced in Jal's mind. Too ill at ease to speak, he stood petrified with his eyes on Eli. Molly and the rest gathered round Eli to greet him.

Jal stole from the room and went upstairs to his bedroom. *These fantastic beings—I need to think. Eli is gigantic. What a day!* The sound of their cheerful conversation and laughter carried up the stairs and seemed to infuse his room with warmth.

In ten minutes or so, he heard Bea come upstairs. After a change of clothes, she knocked on his door and entered. "Is anything wrong, Jal?" She patted his head and examined his face. "Let's hurry down. Eli tells us stories; I'm hungry, and I know you are too. Are you rattled in Eli's presence, Jal? He's a good and gentle being. Wait till you hear his story; then you'll understand."

"He's awesome, so big and golden."

"Yes, he is that! You can sit beside me at dinner. Don't be difficult, please."

"Right-o, Bea, in a minute." He got up and rinsed his face and hands, and then he and Bea went downstairs to the dining room.

He took a chair next to Bea and kept his head lowered until Molly took her seat. The vegetables, corn and fresh beans, a roast, and salad were dispensed the length of the table. Eli smiled and handed a dish to Jal, which he received with a shy, "Thank you." Composed and silent, he listened to the cheerful talk swirling around him.

Eli, questioned about his day's activities, said, "My latest mission has entered a thorny phase. Mediation sessions are on schedule for the next week, and that means I'll have to be present every day to arbitrate matters. I'm booked into the village inn until case closure. The file notes will be available after that. Feel free to read them."

"And that we will," Molly said. "We'll give Luellen an extra-busy office day."

Callie brought in the special dessert and placed a serving before Jal and Sammie. "The treat. Ben's latest concoction. For you, Bea, nectar made from berries by Cecil."

"We've already had a treat; the dinner was so good," Sammie said. "But we never refuse an extra dessert."

"Top notch," Jal decided, spooning the mixture into his mouth.

"And capped off that special apple pie," Sammie added. "Your cooking is A+." She accepted their thanks by giving them another serving.

Bea, unmindful of the two pairs of eyes on her, used a miniature spoon to eat hers.

"Just wait," Sammie whispered to Jal.

Bea, holding her spoon in midair, squeezed her eyes into thin slits, and looked at them.

"Come friends, let us go to the verandah, and share in the gifts of the evening," Eli said after dinner.

Mollie and Callie cleared away with Monty's help and soon joined the group. Jal sat between Bea and Sammie, attending to the flow of the conversation. He leaned over to Sammie, "Where is Missy? Why doesn't she sit with us?"

"In time, give her time."

Dusk descended, unveiling the full luster of moonlight. The stars were out in myriad array. In the buzz of conversation, Jal became conscious of how alone he had felt during the days of his uncle's absence. Gratitude to Syntee and affection for Bea and Sammie welled up within him. His eyes went to Eli and Molly and to each of the group members who had so affectionately accepted him.

The longing for his parents and his uncle shadowed him, ever present. Still, an assurance was growing in his heart that somehow lessened the sting of his pain. His hope of a future reunion was taking on more substance. The words of his mother echoed like the tug on a string drawing her to him: "The cord of love is strong; it threads its way from my heart to your heart."

He shifted his attention outward. Two figures were strolling toward them, one tall and one short. *They must be Cecil and Ben. Cecil is about my height.* They hailed everyone, and Cecil said with a drawl, "We were told our newest immigrant wants to meet us, so here we are. Hallo to you, Jal, welcome to our country."

He replied with thanks meanwhile noting their contrasting appearance. Ben's brown eyes were grave in a face framed by brown, curly hair. His manner was mild and serious and his clothes rumpled. Cecil, with a pale face and straw-colored hair, was dressed nattily in a dark blue suit and tie. Witty and chatty, he blended glibly into the currents of the conversation.

The group talked of daily happenings until the dusk deepened and the mauve shadows grew dense.

"How is Missy?" Eli inquired of Molly during a lull in the chatter.

"Everyone agrees she's a dear, and her self-confidence is growing with each assignment. She likes the baking in particular and lunches with Callie and me. Within a week or two, she'll be talking everyone's ear off and joining us for dinner. She sings during the day in a beautiful soprano voice. Porter is trying mightily to recruit her for his band. It won't be long; we know our persistent Porter."

Callie added, "And she will lend a hand tomorrow; it's baking day. She's quite lively with Molly and me, actually a chatterbox. She's feeling more at ease with Porter and Monty this past week."

A cute face looked out from the dining room window. *She must be Missy. She's like the little eyes in the underbrush.* She smiled at him and then moved away.

Porter commented with a chuckle, "Persistence pays off, just as the trees do in growing their fruit. Missy will be part of the band before the fall ends. And speaking of baking…the orchards took up most of my day. Lots of pies and cobblers to be on the menu at harvest time, Molly."

"My time to barge in. I chug away like Porter. I completed a round of patrols; the north section today," Monty said. "A week's work."

"Excellent. Your diligence is remarkable, Monty." His face lit up at Eli's praise.

Bea whispered to Jal, "Porter is the manager of Eli's estate. He's also an outstanding musician. Monty's farm duties are special. I'll tell you his story later."

Jal said to her with a droll grin, "There are oodles of 'tell me laters' to do."

"You...I know what you are. You're a...what is it...oh, yes; you're a wagwit. Go figure that out, you exasperating thing." She sniffed.

Molly, smiling, got up from her chair and touched Sammie on his shoulder. "The three of you will be off in early morning, so to sleep for the young one."

Eli said he had some office work to do and got to his feet. "Soon we're having a get together, Jal, and you'll be here with Grandfather Moutyn. My travels may bring me your way before then." He exchanged good nights and went inside.

Ben and Cecil moved off the verandah to the lawn.

Jal set off after them. "Cecil, Ben, wait a minute. Sammie told me your story, Cecil, a riveting tale. I'd like to hear more. May I visit you and the place where you work?"

"Anytime, Jal. You will be a favored guest. Send a note when you're ready. I'll tell you whatever you want to know about the Kulkuks."

"Cecil and I live in the research facility; we each have an apartment, plenty of room to share with you, Jal. We'll show you over the buildings, and we'll confess the secrets of our work," Ben said.

Jal kept them in his sight as they crossed the moonlit lawn, their lengthened shadows behind them. *Like a queue,* he thought. *Terrific fellows.*

Porter lived in a large stone house on the opposite side of the stream. He pointed in its direction and said, "Bea and Sammie stay over on occasions. I want you to visit the family, Jal. Get settled in with Grandfather Moutyn and plan for a long weekend break. Come meet the gang. We have an assortment of nephews and nieces about your age. You might like to get acquainted with the musician chaps also."

Jal weighed Porter's words while his eyes searched his genial face, "You're very kind, Porter; I'll cruise in one day. Do you think I could squeeze in a night's stay with Cecil and Ben?"

"Of course, Jal, no problem."

On his way upstairs with Bea and Sammie, Jal said, "That was most gratifying, to quote Mom after our family outings."

"A suitable session for the three of us. Goodnight, you two, sleep tight. I'm cruising off to bed. Carry on, Sammie." Bea glided into her room.

Sammie said, "You've twigged to why Bea and I are partial to the gatherings. See you in the morning, Jal."

"Sammie, my feet aren't as tired today. These are fifty-miles-a-day shoes. What a neat group they are—I mean Eli's family circle. Good night, Sammie." Jal hastily entered his room and closed the door.

He completed his washing up, tumbled into bed, and reviewed the day. His troubles receded into a distant past. The two days with Bea and Sammie were creating new experiences to tuck into his memory collection. *Mom is going to say, 'Jal, if you're making up stories record them on your RI.' Maybe the staggering ones anyhow. Another fun day.* He dropped off to sleep and to dream of past happy times with his parents and his uncle.

Third Day
10

Jal awoke to a sweet aroma wafting up from the kitchen. Bea and Sammie entered the room, dressed and ready for the day's journey.

"Umm—umm, get a whiff of that." Bea snuffled, wrinkling her tiny nose. "Hurry up, Jal, I'm half starved. The heavenly fragrance we smell is a cup of cocoa for you. We'll wait for you to shower and dress."

"I guess I better hurry. I don't want to stand between you and your half hunger," Jal said on his way into the bathroom. "I'll be right out."

On the stairs, Bea planted a kiss on his head. "Thanks for being prompt, you thoughtful boy."

Mollie was bustling about at the dining room table. "Sit and eat a leisurely breakfast. Eli is already off on his day's mission. Monty and Porter are meeting with the staff at the dairy farm this morning. Anyhow, we're verging on our next get-together."

Callie came in from the kitchen and put freshly made blueberry pancakes on Jal's plate. He nibbled on one gingerly and said, "These are super—the first ones I've eaten since Uncle Joulh and I left home. Mom made them for Dad and me on Sunday mornings." He took a drink of his frothy cocoa and a bite of his sausage. "I used to love cherry crepes best, but now I don't. My loathing list got a tack on the morning Dad told me about his and Mom's military bit."

Bea smacked her lips while sipping her fruit nectar and voiced her understanding. "Just like I can't stand eating from grass flowers after my summer's horror."

Sammie gave him a pat on the hand and made sounds of approval while savoring his grains. "Cherry crepes were never a favorite of mine; I'll take grains any day."

"A good breakfast is needed for a day's journey; you three fill up before starting out," Molly said.

"Yes, do," Callie said. "Travel stirs the appetite; we don't want you to be hungry."

"I do too. I agree about the fill up; I get grumpy when I'm hungry," Bea piped up.

Jal ogled her, widening his eyes into brown marbles. "We know you like a good breakfast. Don't we, Sammie?"

"You two young'uns," she groaned. "Whatever am I going to do with you? I saw you two conspirators whispering at dinner last night. And your subject was me."

Sammie and Jal grinned without comment.

Jal went upstairs straightaway after breakfast and folded his clothes from the day before. He left them on the bed with the thought, *A thank you to Molly; Mom liked me to fold my clothes.* He went downstairs, ready to go.

"Missy packed an extra snack and lunch for the three of you. Here it is," Callie said and handed Sammie a paper bag.

Sammie stuck his head in the living room doorway. "Thanks, Missy."

She peeked out from the kitchen and said, "Welcome."

Molly went to the end of the graveled walkway with them and waited until they reached the path. They waved a farewell to her and to Missy, whom they spied standing on the verandah. "Next time she won't be so shy, will she, Sammie, and I won't be either?"

"Probably not, Jal, but it's best to let her adjust in her own way."

"On today's walk, the saga of the Dilydalys might tempt your thoughtful propensities. The tale of Eli is on offer to mollify your pining for a story this morning. "

"Please, Sammie, tell me; he's fabulous, a fabutale. Eli is so awesome, but he's friendly. I intend to be friendlier when he talks to me next time. Everyone I've met is splendid. Just think—I might have missed this! Before you tell the story, let's walk and listen to the birds. They do gabble a lot, don't they?"

Bea replied, "They natter the daylong. Perhaps we'll get another song from the stream and a chorus of warblings. A morning symphony, you might say.

"To speak of the residents you're meeting, Jal...Sammie and I are introducing you to our very dear friends. We're happy you like them. They will be your friends, present and future. This specific path was chosen for you by Syntee."

"Yes, it was. I cheer that statement," Sammie added.

"I like walking this path," Jal said after a period of silence. "At home we went walking in the park. This is much better."

He caught a glimpse of bright, beady eyes poking out from the underbrush. The babblings of the stream were low key and the melodic tones restrained. A few birds and animals were drinking from a pool bordered with yellow wild flowers.

"The stream's gift to them, I suppose," he said aloud.

"Hah?" Bea said.

"I'm learning from you two." He laughed and pointed to the assembly of creatures at the pool.

Their steps slowed to observe the colorful display.

"They don't seem to object to sharing," Jal observed.

"No, an example for us all," Bea replied.

"Maybe someone should tell the ones who started the war," Jal said wryly.

"A vexing issue, Jal. It's had a go; put it by for another day. I'll begin Eli's story, if you're ready."

Jal filed his thoughts away. "Sure, Sammie, I'm on standby. Ready, set..."

"The chronicle of Eli opens like this. His parents were royalty, and being the eldest son, he was in line to be the future king. His country is very old; I mean the one in which he was born. Its lineage of kings, the dynasty Aribasleh, stretches into infinity. Eli's brother, Athos, is the youngest in the family. An only sister, Anastasia, is married to Prince Bertrand Millardo of an adjoining country. Eli says his travels their way are increasing in frequency which denotes growth of his missions.

"Eli trained during his youth and young adulthood to acquire the requisites of ruling the kingdom. He undertook his rigorous assignments obediently and without protest but with a divided heart. The prospect of being king carried a tinge of sadness he couldn't explain to himself. At eighteen years of age, his father appointed him court minister to the kingdom's subjects.

"He traveled within his country as a magistrate, mediating conflicts and interceding on behalf of the helpless. He discovered his gift for ministering to others and in the process, a love for travel. Whenever his duties permitted, he did a disappearing act, to the chagrin of his parents.

"Dressed in the simple, everyday clothes of his subjects, he toured his country and the world, incognito. Somewhere before his twenty-first birthday, he encountered Syntee. The how and where they met is unknown. We intend to ask Syntee when we have our leisure time in the spring."

Jal interrupted, "You do know a lot though, Sammie. Did Syntee tell you? How do you know so much?"

"Secret stories are rare in this country. If a citizen prefers privacy, the record notes it, but the story is available to Syntee's messengers. The sharing is often helpful to new immigrants. That will apply to yours also, Jal.

"To proceed...Eli's parents held a strong wish to retire to their country estate, the epicenter of their philanthropic projects. They were more than ready for Eli's ascension to the throne. Still they kept an eye on his activities through the years with growing uneasiness. They valued his gentleness and kindness and thought he would learn to love his sovereign role. 'In any case,' his mother said, 'a good king helps his subjects when there is need. Eli has the esteem of our citizens; he will be a noble monarch.'

"The time approached for Eli to assume the throne. However, he was more depressed than ever at the thought of it. His parents were distraught as they observed his despondency. 'We can't go on like this, seeing our son so unhappy,' his mother said to the king.

"They conferred with a trusted court advisor who recommended they meet with Eli to sort out the issues. A short time later, his mother set a date to discuss coronation activities. Eli, after a sleepless night of fretting, entered his parents' private chamber on the morning of the appointment. Determined to reveal his long-held aspirations, his father forestalled him.

"Immediately, the king began, 'Eli, let's forget the coronation for a minute. We've been conscious of your growing discontent during the past two years and your dreadfully low spirits. Our hearts have been heavy with sorrow ever since we became aware of your unhappiness. At first, we thought it was just a phase, a passing mood. Give us an answer, son. Why this wretched gloom of yours? What is the basis of your despondency? Whatever the source surely you can tell us.'

"Eli got up and moved to a window that faced the street below. An ornate iron fence walled off the palace grounds. At the gated entrance, ten guards stood attired in brightly colored uniforms.

"He came near to his parents and said, 'Your love gives me the courage to tell you of my feelings this morning. Our palace with its pomp and royal ceremonies is isolated from the teeming lives of our citizens. To live apart as a confined ruler to this state is intolerable to me. The power to benefit the inhabitants of the world lies within my grasp. Only you can free me to follow the vision that propels me toward a greater destiny than this kingdom.

"Father, both you and Mother recognize the administrative abilities of Athos, even though he's still quite young. He would be an able king, devoted to his duties. I'll do whatever you consider best until he completes his training.'

"His father brought the hand of the queen to his lips. 'It pains us exceedingly, Eli, but we won't stand in your way. We care for you too much to forbid a course of action you are determined on. We are aware that Athos is adept and clever. We had hopes…Eli. At your request, a command to release you from your duties goes forth. Just don't forget the ones who love you more than all the kingdoms of the world.'

"'Forget you, the best of parents?' Eli replied. 'I promise to keep in touch; I'll come in often for a visit. An app for communicating will be shared with you. I can be reached at any hour by its use. Thank you for your understanding and support. I would be a most ungrateful son if ever I forgot your loving care.'

"Free to plan his future, Eli soon arranged with Syntee to be a chief messenger. Athos was crowned king three years later. And so, dream fulfilled–Eli keeps his promise to his parents. He introduced them to Syntee, and they shared His teachings with their kingdom. Now quite old, they live on their country estate and actively promote this country's work. King Athos has reigned for a number of years, 'an excellent king,' Eli says with affection."

With a flourish and a bow, Sammie ended the story.

"Sammie, that's a grand story, like another fabutale, except it's in reverse. This time the prince didn't gain a kingdom; he gave one up. I don't know if I could give up a kingdom for this country. Eli must know more than anyone knows and be great—the greatest in the world to be Syntce's chief messenger. Do you think, Sammie, Eli would teach me?"

"A real possibility, Jal. Store it in your cache of things to do. Once you and Grandfather Moutyn work out a preliminary schedule, you might reopen the topic."

"Does everyone in Eli's household have a story too?"

"Certainly they do, and I'll tell you more after lunch. Let me see; Missy is new. The details of her life aren't released yet. Her given name is Louisa Victoria. Montague, Molly, and Callie? We've time to tell you theirs."

"Please, a requester I am. I do like the stories, Sammie."

"There are loads of others that you'll learn in good time," Bea said.

11

The morning by this time was far advanced, and Jal became conscious of being hungry. The path curved in an upward sweep, and the babbling stream rushed down an incline in foamy sprays. The sun sparkled and danced on the vaporous water. Glittering particles of light like glass bubbles swirled about his feet. *Little stars on the ground, I'm walking on little stars.* He opened his mouth to tell Bea just as Sammie said, "We'll eat our lunch here if you two are hungry."

"Yes, let's; I have a voracious hunger. I'm splitting for a seat, guys," Bea said.

Jal caught up with her when she touched down on a stone bench. "I was hypnotized by Eli's story and forgot lunch. You seem to be hungry a lot. You say it so often." He chuckled while marveling at the beauty of her outspread wings. "I'm starved too, I admit."

"You're an impertinent young'un," she snapped, rapping him on the head.

"Ow," Jal said, rubbing his head. "For a tiny creature, you have a mighty rap."

"Hey! Behave yourself, or two raps will be your lot," she said and settled again on the three-seater stone bench.

Sammie handed a sandwich to Jal made of multigrain bread and a white cheese. "From Eli's farm," he said, giving him a fruit and a vegetable with a container of milk. Bea took a little earthenware pot filled with nectar.

"This is extra special," Jal said in a garbled tone while taking a bite of his sandwich.

"Mine is so great; would you like a sample? I shouldn't give you any since you made the crack about my endless hunger. You'll get why I'm a fervent eater. The best nectar is brewed on Eli's farm."

"And the best grains," Sammie added.

Jal took the pot and detected a flavor of jasmine in the honey. "Ooo...um, so good; I think I'll down it to the last drop."

"No, no, you don't." She snatched at the pot. "Quit your teasing, Jal, or I'll take you in hand, you aggravating thing." She offered Sammie a taste.

"Yes," Sammie said, "delish, just like my grains. Delectable grains are cultivated on Eli's farm. Ben and Cecil are creative in coming up with different varieties. I try a new one every time we visit."

"Let me tack this on, Jal," Bea said. "You've scoped out the source of our food, grown on the farms of our hospitable hosts.

You'll meet another farmer in a day or two. Remember when I said, 'Be patient, and you'll learn.'"

"Yes, I do, and marked off as learning. I still have a lot more questions!"

"Wait."

"You say that in batches. I bet I'll hear the stream babbling the words pretty soon."

"You might as well give up; evermore we're waiting on some question to be answered."

"Might as well get off the subject then," he replied.

"You two make for a merry day, but time to go," Sammie cut in.

"I must say," Jal said as they stepped onto the path, "I can walk farther now without being so tired. I was really done in that first day."

"Yep, reminded me of a ragamuffin, limp as a rag and fit to drop," Bea replied. "Needless to say, I don't have to walk. I get a free ride—pickaback."

Jal stopped and began to laugh.

"What? I'm not that funny. Jokey possibly, but not hilarious," Bea said, waving her antennae at him.

"A thought just came to me; a good thing I wasn't completely worn out the first day. Just think—Sammie might have had to carry me."

"Then I would have been pickaback on your head."

They both laughed.

"Stop this nonsense," Sammie chided in a stern voice.

"Yes, boss," Bea replied in a formal tone and rolled her eyes in imitation of Sammie. She and Jal laughed again.

Sammie shook his head. "A comedy duo in a riotous act, ha-ha...but now to the story of the Dilydalys, another riotous act."

"Who are the Dilydalys?" Jal asked.

"The Dilydalys?" Bea said. "Why they are—Sammie, please, you tell him their story."

Sammie, amused at her discomfort, said, "Bea never likes to tell this story."

"The Dilydalys dreamed of creating their own country, or more properly a colony. They worked diligently to devise ways to prolong their leisure time. 'Creative and inventive time,' they styled it. For your info, Jal, the Kulkuks, the Dazidazlers, and the Dilydalys lived in the same time span, an era of excessive affluence. These three organized groups were survivors of many factions formed during the same period. A significant time indeed! Democracy as a form of government was in decline due to infighting. Everyone did what was expedient in their own eyes.

"This all happened more than a hundred years ago, round 2060 to 2070. The WC evolved and assumed world governance in about 2073. Four districts spanned the globe: Southern, Northern, Eastern, and Western.

"Anyhow, several things cropped up in the last century: the defeat of a dangerous enemy that threatened world destruction and the WC's development. The eradication of advanced war armaments a few years later is of vital importance. The whole earth cheered that one! Plans, designs, and documentation pertaining to the weapons were obliterated, even to the erasure of archived documents. The antique weapons, guns, tanks, etc., became museum pieces. The WC, guided by a set of life principles, ushered in an age of peace. Moreover, the world's inhabitants elected to conserve and preserve the environment. As a result, these acts led to a more modest lifestyle. Sound like your studies?"

"Yes, I've studied history for three years. I learned the Principles for a United World, or the PUW, at seven. Dad examined my work every week to be certain I understood their meaning."

"To quit the digressing..." Sammie said. "The old practice of grouping people by ethnicity was abolished. Resettlement and migration was encouraged across the four districts. English became the official language as most countries spoke it at the time. Then, certain restraints encroached on individual and group freedom for the collective good. An important PUW tenet states that individual liberty must be expressed within the framework of social responsibility.

"The control of public and private media followed accordingly. Neighborhood tech centers filled in for the personal loss of computers, phones, reading devices, and other techy gizmos. National transport became the norm. Naturally, the importance of the bicycle ballooned in favor with the villagers."

"Yes, I have one, Sammie. Uhlin and I often ride them on errands. Though Mom doesn't allow me to use the airlift."

"A vigilant mom. Airlifts are locked until you're sixteen," Bea said.

"On our subject..." Sammie said. "Another principal tenet is the dismissal of any belief in a divine being. The Executive Branch of the WC considers religion superfluous. Religion leads to fanaticism is the general supposition. Its practice is discouraged but isn't prohibited outright. A crafty campaign to suppress sacred books and literature has succeeded uncommonly well. The practitioners keep a low profile and attend meetings in their homes."

"Sammie, I know what you're doing. You're tossing in a history lesson. I like the subject, a favorite of mine. But there's no mention of religion in my history readings.

"I remember Mom telling me that our government appropriated church buildings for office use when my grandmother was a child. Do you know if they were, Sammie?"

"Yes, I do. The government took the buildings to house their employees. The exterior of the structures weren't altered, thus the beauty remains. The only new building erected was the peerless tower, HQ of the WC, which draws the world's veneration.

"Syntee says His work has increased since the WC restricted religious teachings. The affair will undoubtedly be on your civics list. And you'll learn about our Book of Authority.

"Anyway, the nations that seceded from the WC learned and applied the techniques of the Savants by cruel means. Weapons, based on the antique models of war, were secretly produced and stockpiled. The age of peace, knotty and frayed, was ending. To make a long story short, it went bust in the global war.

'To go back to our story...the Dilydalys searched for a suitable location, one that would give them the freedom to pursue their creativity. They found an isolated place among tree-clad hills, well watered and fertile. As you'll witness, Jal, their plants and gardens grew with little effort. Content in growing their edibles and weaving beautiful cloth, they prospered with leisure in abundance. They built up a thriving trade in colorful garments and home furnishings. Their inventions were almost as prolific as the bountiful crops—inventions meant to promote greater ease."

"Sammie, I get bored when I have time to myself, even time off from my studies. I wonder why they worked so hard to ditch work."

"Befuddlement is your answer, Jal. Postpone wonderings until the viewing.

"After the first generation grew old and the next one assumed power, a shift in outlook occurred. They were less industrious and more prone to engage in amusements. A hefty portion of their leisure went to the inventions of entertainment. By the third generation…incomparable and zany sights!"

Jal opened his mouth to ask a question and felt a rap on his head. Bea said, "Just wait, you'll see."

They walked in silence, listening to the sounds in the woods until the path rounded an angled bend. The air grew balmy and refreshing, and Jal removed his jacket and tied it round his waist. Taking note of the pleasant trickling of the stream, he was content to wait. A wide arc then precipitated them into an appalling racket. Jal put his hands over his ears and viewed the rowdy scene.

Figures were in the air, swooping and diving with astounding speed. Others hovered above the ground on what appeared to be cushions. A group scrambled to catch a square object that evaded their grasp by leaping from side to side. *Odd,* Jal thought, *like a ricocheting boomerang.* On walking further, he saw a luxuriant garden bordered by a low wall made of stone. Purple and blue flowering trees grew in unruly profusion.

"Here we are at Ezelan," Bea said. "Such fun; it's a ball, it's a blast. What do you say?"

"I don't know, Bea. What are they doing? Looks silly to me."

"Whatnots, Jal. You're watching organized activities. The Dilydalys value this way of life."

The noise grew louder. A trio seemed to be in a spat, pushing and shoving each other.

A group of four jumped back and forth over the wall with concentrated effort. No one responded when Jal said hello. They ignored him in the unruly deafening racket.

"The Dilydalys find outsiders repugnant," Sammie said, observing Jal's quizzical eyes.

"They're not the only ones. I find the insiders, if that's what they call themselves, repugnant," Jal replied.

"I say, Bea, it's taking an awfully long time to pass them," he said with a puckered brow.

She sensed his thoughts and said. "I say, time does seem to expand when we're obliged to watch activities we don't like. Sort of like me having to watch a race."

"We can say that fifty times and more," Jal replied in a vexed tone. "It's interminable. Mom said whenever Dad and I were watching a game of soccer, 'Will this interminable game never end?' And I can tell you, Bea, I was about three years old when I last played a jumping game. No fun for me in seeing a baby game."

"Did you hear him, Sammie? A baby game indeed! The dear child is a comedian."

"And feeling a tad underfed. Right about now I could use the snack Molly gave us."

"I'm ready any old time," Bea said, heading to the stream. "Here's a pretty spot, a seat big enough for three."

Sammie took his pouch off and reached inside. "Our treat, an apricot nectar for Bea, a crepe of three cheeses for you and the three-grain mix I love. Callie's fresh creation this morning."

"Sammie, I'm glad Callie gave me this crepe. The last one Mom fixed for me spoilt my taste for crepes, but it wasn't the crepes' fault. This one is yummy."

"Very good, Jal. An unexpected bonus in a Callie special."

"But don't give me any cherry crepes yet. I'll have to wait and see before I eat another one," he said with a mischievous glint in his eyes.

"We will remember, won't we, Bea?"

"Yes, no cherry crepes. To the trail now, Sammie. Yummy lunch ahead."

"Woo-woo, lunch, she says." Jal made munching sounds.

"You keep your tongue in your mouth, Jal Valhyn. Impossible scamp of a boy!" she snapped.

12

Back on the path, an expanse of trees looping the stream in a semicircle obscured the view. On ascending a rise, the trees left off, and the hills folded like pleats in the far-off distance. The scene struck a chord within him, and Jal voiced his thoughts to Sammie and Bea.

"You know, Bea and Sammie, this place reminds me of a picnic…I was about three or four years old. My memories are somewhat vague, but Mom, Dad, and Uncle Joulh are playing a game of ball with me. I feel a little sad at the memory. Why is that?"

"You're missing your loved ones. The view from here triggers a remembrance of happy events and causes the feeling," Sammie replied. "It's well to have the memories, Jal. A prized artifact to store in your memory cache, as we might say."

Bea said, "We treasure the good things, and we learn to live with the sad things. Syntee taught us this. I've had a fair amount of sad experiences. I don't count the drought summer. That's my season of realized ambitions.

"In time your views and understanding will broaden and deepen. The present events are timely in honing those very skills."

"I agree with that statement. Wait and see," Sammie said.

Jal nodded his head. "The cache of these 'wait and sees' you and Bea are giving me is getting bigger. Before we get to Grandfather Moutyn's, I'll need a packhorse to carry them."

He pondered on their remarks and said, "Funny you should mention storing memories, Sammie. I stored a memory away, the one I treasure most." He quoted his mother's words, "'The cord of love is strong.' I do so miss Mom and Dad."

Jal tugged at his backpack, and said. "Will I ever be as brave as you, Sammie?"

"A plucky spirit like you, Jal, I expect you may, if not already. We're born into a world where sorrows and woes are in ample supply. So the hurts come along with the territory. We each get a portion—no escaping. Life makes us equal in that! Troubles are like fires, floods, and droughts. The trio swamped you with a cramming course for the navigation of all three.

"But Jal, no matter how our troubles originate, we can use them in the construction of a sturdy inner edifice, or we can live a defeated life. Each hurt can be recycled into a unit for our building. Think of it like a brick. In time, an inner structure mortared by compassion can materialize to withstand the greatest of storms. Compassion is a highly valued characteristic in this country, a basic accessory if we aspire to help others. Bea and I would be poor messengers indeed if we hadn't learned the lesson."

Jal inhaled deeply and breathed out by degrees. "Dad and Uncle Joulh told me endless times to have courage and to fight the dragons. Are you talking about dragons, Sammie?"

"Yes, I am. Troubles are just another name for the dragons seeking to defeat us. There's more to learn but time enough to learn 'the more.' Little by little, our learning advances."

"Never fear, Jal, it does," Bea said. "Loads of help is on offer to fight the dragons in this country. And to build an inner edifice. Take heart—you are quite a speedy learner. Consider me. A poor specimen I was before an extravagant darling took me in hand."

Jal mulled over Sammie and Bea's words. At length, the dwindling light reminded him of the passing day. On the horizon, the faint outline of the crescent moon indicated the approach of evening. He became aware of being hungry and tired. He looked at Bea, who had closed her eyes and was bobbing about on Sammie's head.

"Woops," she yelled, "a goner for sure. Aren't we at the cabin yet, Sammie? I went to sleep just now."

"Not long, Bea, hold on for a few more minutes."

Jal listened to them with an inward chuckle. "Thank you, Sammie and Bea, for being my friends," he said.

Sammie replied, "It's mutual, Jal; we're pleased to be your friends."

They reached the guesthouse at sunset. The cabin's design was similar to the previous one. Three rocking chairs on the porch that were placed between the two windows appeared inviting.

"One for Papa Bear, one for Mama Bear, and one for Baby Bear," Bea said.

"Yes, indeed," Sammie said, giving Jal a grin, "We'll sit in them after dinner and contemplate our witty companion."

Bea opened her eyes wide in circular motions. "I can't help it, being witty. A natural trait. You're excused from tonight's adulation. Perchance another evening."

"Thank you, oh great wit. Your adoring twosome is ready for feeding. Your deal is accepted," Sammie replied.

A bedroom with two single beds and a bathroom comprised the interior. Clothes for the night and the next day hung from pegs on the wall. A white mini cabinet opposite their beds contained Bea's room. The food, in red paper bags and three white plates, sat on a red-and-white-checked kitchen table. Flatware and three trays were on a low cabinet with jars of milk and fruit drinks.

"Now for the porridge. And look, someone has been ultra-considerate, matching the colors!" Bea said.

"We can each leave a note of thanks this time," Sammie added.

"A dip in the stream before eating?" Bea asked with a towel in her hand.

After a lap of swimming, Sammie and Jal splashed each other in fun.

"Not me, now don't splash me," Bea scolded. "Don't you two muss my hair!"

"Muss your hair?" Jal said with wide eyes. "What hair?"

"Jal Valhyn, you know you can see my hair, behave yourself," Bea retorted.

Sammie laughed. "Never get into a tussle with Bea about her hair. She wins every time. A lesson I learned by an aching head."

Jal smiled at Bea and said to Sammie, "Ready or not, here I go."

They raced each other to the cabin. "I won," Bea said, soaring into the room.

"Not fair." Jal replied, "You can fly while we have to run on legs."

"Too, too bad for you. Sometimes we win, and sometimes we lose. This was my time to win."

They placed their food on the trays and carried them to the porch.

"The baby one is mine," Bea said and sat on the arm of the chair.

"Ah...hh," she exhaled noisily, "yellow nectar."

"Delectable grains," Sammie added from his papa chair.

Jal nodded his head and rocked forward in his mama chair. "To quote Bea, I do agree. This black bread and lentil soup is pippin' good."

They sat in silent attention as the crescent moon ascended higher in the heavens.

"Like it's being pushed by an unseen hand," Bea remarked.

The night's cool air closed about them like an embrace, and in the darkness, a mass of shining stars became visible.

"See the evening star," Sammie said, pointing to the most brilliant star. "A performance that I never grow tired of."

"I never knew the night could be friendly," Jal said. "Two new subjects to learn, Sammie, the stars and the night."

"The presentation of the heavens is a boundless study, Jal, but even more is the awareness of its beauty."

"Windfall of the heavens. And speaking of awareness, time to think of bedtime," Bea said.

"Everyone must be asleep by now," Jal said.

"Yes," Sammie said. "The birds and the ground creatures call it a day at twilight. Early to bed, early to rise."

"I would like to know who said that first," Bea mused. "There are night creatures, but we aren't much acquainted with them since we work during the day. I've listened to the owls say, whoo—whoo in the night. Reminds me of the time I said to Syntee, 'Who...who...are you?'" They laughed together.

She went on, "Bats are curious creatures of the night. One time I heard a story of how they share a cave with birds. They exchange at nightfall, when the bats fly out the birds fly in. Works without a glitch for their sleeping habits. I would like to see that. But for now—time for creatures such as we to be in bed."

With a glint in his eyes, Jal said, "The Nitecraulers—"

"You stop right there," Bea said. "Never mention those horrors to me. We're going to bed."

"Okay, Bea, but my joke's gone missing."

"Chase it some other day. We're closing this banter."

Nightly tasks were soon completed, and minutes later they were snug in their beds. Jal reviewed his day, and a vague memory came to him of a conversation he had overheard. *I'll ask Sammie and Bea about it.* He put the thought into his query cache and sank into restful slumber.

Fourth Day
13

Jal awoke to the morning light streaming through the window. Refreshed and eager to begin the day's journey, he popped out of bed and into the bathroom.

Sammie, putting their lunch into his rucksack for the day, said, "Good morning, my lad."

"Ready to eat," Bea said. "I'll try to wait until you shower. Better hurry up."

"Okay, Bea. Don't munch mine, you ravenous thing. Give me time to put my clothes on. Be there in a minute." He showered, dressed, and came to the table.

"I'm hungry this morning. Seconds are my clamoring cry. Or I might devour your nectar and Sammie's grains."

"Hey, just try it, you exasperating thing," Bea replied. "Preposterous boy, moocher! There's loads of food for you. Imagine! Saying I'm ravenous."

"Umm—umm, so good. I like the word ravenous, Bea. I do like to eat—I mean this food."

"You speak for me, Jal," Sammie said with a grin.

"Add me," Bea said. "I do relish my nectar, but not to a ravenous degree."

Sammie took paper and pen from the cabinet and said, "We do agree that the note I'm writing will include our thanks for the food that fills our avid appetites?" He lifted his eyes, and then smiled at them.

After an added thanks to the note, Jal finished off the breakfast chores. Sammie picked up their lunch, and in next to no time, they were on their way. Jal gazed at Bea perched on Sammie's head. A sense of admiration filled him as Sammie moved into a patch of sunlight. Bea's colors flamed iridescently for a minute. *Just like my whirligig spinning. Funny, I don't miss the whirligig anymore. Guess I've outgrown toys.* Gladdened by this thought, he transferred his attention to the terrain.

"What's up for today?" he asked.

"Today," Bea said, "we'll reach Bogie's farm. We'll stay the night with Bogart and Olivia, a.k.a., Bogie and Ollie to everyone in this country."

"Please, would you tell me their story?"

"After the morning charms us with its favors. Aren't you a wee bit tired of the tales?"

"No I'm not; I could listen to your stories for ever so long. A day's study left me in tatters, but not your stories."

"In tatters, eh?" Bea said. "I'd better get to the saga."

They slowed their steps to observe the activities of the creatures in the underbrush and the ever-changing landscape. Overnight, it seemed, the leaves had taken on a dash of the yellows and reds of autumn. The sun tipped the trees and spilled in slivers of light upon the path. The stream gushed in bubbly waterfalls down a smooth slate rock.

"How picturesque. A fine home for the birds and ground creatures."

"And for us, Bea," Jal said. "Break is over. On to our story?"

"A demand not to be refused by a cheering audience," Sammie said.

"It all began in the Northern division of the WC where Ollie and Bogie grew up. They lived on neighboring farms and had loved each other since childhood. Rumors of a possible war with a neighboring country were a minor concern in their everyday life. The WC, in negotiation with the parties in question, would without doubt resolve the problems. The reports of progress relieved the fears voiced by a few citizens.

"However, to their alarm, the enemy struck unexpectedly. Bogie, ordered to the frontlines of battle, put marriage on the shelf. The failure of the WC to reign in the rebel nations unleashed a war that shattered hopes of world unity.

"And By the way, Jal, the war has endured for many long years. Bogie's country chucked neutrality for combat within a year of the war rumors. Yours did six months ago. In fact, your former country, the headquarters of the WC, was the final one to enter the fracas."

"Why do you say 'your former country,' Sammie? You said that before in one of the stories you told me."

"I use the phrase a lot, don't I? I'll explain. When you heard and obeyed Syntee's instructions, you began a journey to a special country or kingdom. Either term will do. Once over the meadow and the stream, you signed on as a citizen. Not an onerous policy?"

"No, doesn't seem to be, but how will Mom and Dad and my Uncle Joulh join me?"

"Trust Syntee, Jal, to handle the details. You'll be a united family in the near future. You can expect your uncle's arrival any day after his military duties end. Rely on Syntee's word. You won't be disappointed."

"Okay, Sammie, but Syntee may have trouble getting Dad here. He was forever saying we were to be loyal to our own country."

"We'll trust Syntee to sign him on. Don't fret. Your father will gladly consent to immigration on learning the ins and outs of his son's new home.

"Now, let's summarize the story of Bogie and Ollie. The enemy's trained military recruits rapidly defeated Bogie's inexperienced armed forces. In short, he was taken captive. The shock of discovering Ollie and her parents, plus his, in the prison camp made him ill. The enemy had seized their village three weeks after he had set out for the front. The farms were impounded and the residents imprisoned.

"Their parents survived only a few months in the prison setting. Bogie recovered his health, and less than a year later, he and Ollie escaped from the camp. With the aid of a sympathetic family, they hid in the countryside until someone contacted Eli. Taken to his farm, they were married within a month. Bea and I were disappointed to miss the gala, but our missions take priority.

"Their greatest wish was to recreate the life they knew and loved. Eli convinced Syntee to send them to the farm where they now live. The former residents emigrated to the home country of Syntee. To be neighbors with Eli, whom they had grown to love, completed their happiness, Ollie said, when she related their story to us. That is the brief outline of their life, Jal.

"In addition to managing a large farm and dairy, they host travelers along this way. Bea and I prize our visits with the family. Twins, Alistair and Bo, are fourteen years old. Twins, Mae and Ada, are twelve years old. Ora, the youngest, is ten years old. Best described as a whirlwind, she has subsided into a small tempest of late. Growing older, no doubt. The five are sparklers of cordiality and welcomes."

Jal listened in silence to Sammie's recitation. He reflected on the story while they walked. *The war did them in with troubles aplenty.* "Sammie, did it take ages for Bogie and Ollie to be happy after their troubles?"

"Feelings related to grief and loss are sorted out and lessen over time. Healing for Bogie and Ollie stemmed from their love for each other and Syntee's guidance. Your answer to the question will be complete when you meet them. Bea and I are proof to being happy. We prefer to call it joy in this country. In the home country of Syntee, my Neda waits for me. Troubles will end when we emigrate to his country. So until then, mis-sioners and ministers we will be, Bea and I."

"Let's eat lunch a mite early, please," Bea interjected. "You two must be tired out and hungry from talking so much."

"Tired out," Jal said. "I don't know about that, but I do know who's hungry."

"I admit I am, and tired. I'm beat from sitting on Sammie's head."

Sammie gave Jal a wide smile and said to Bea, who was standing on the tip of his beak, "Not long now, Bea. Lunch is in the offing."

"I get cranky when I'm hungry, Sammie, so do make it fast." She sprang into the air and vanished round a bend.

"Look at her, Sammie. She uses you as a blast-off pad," Jal said.

"So she does," Sammie replied in a good-humored tone. "That's Bea."

14

In the curve of the stream carpeted by grass and minute red flowers, Sammie spoke. "A charming rest stop. We'd better take a break, or Bea will be tapping on my head all afternoon."

She ignored him with a frown on her face as she settled on a flower. Then she flew to a large flat stone to drink her nectar. Sammie and Jal took a seat on each side of her as they ate in leisurely comfort. Jal savored the flavors of dried apples, a grain veggie burger, and chocolate milk.

"There's something about this food—it has a different yummy taste every day. I like to take my time eating."

Sammie nodded while munching his mixed grains.

"I want to learn how it's done. I'll ask Porter when I visit him," Jal added.

Bea put her nectar down on the rock without speaking. She crinkled up her face and narrowed her eyes at them several times.

Paying no heed, they talked past her and ate. "Yes, Porter loves to talk in detail about his work. When you learn, memo me," Sammie replied.

"The creatures aren't stirring. Maybe they're having lunch too," Jal said while he observed Bea's fidgety movements.

Bea wrinkled her nose and darted to the flower again. She sat blending into its rich colors and muttering to herself. Jal, fascinated, peeked at her sideways through his fingers. Her mutters grew louder. Sammie disregarded her and went on eating. They were halfway through their lunch when she spoke in a pacifying tone. "This place is really pretty, Sammie."

In accord, Jal and Sammie caroled, "Welcome, Bea."

Sammie patted the seat and motioned to her. "We felt quite abandoned without your prattle."

She flew to the rock, picked up her nectar, and gave a sigh of satisfaction as the last bit disappeared. "Ahh…a soother. I'm now ready for our p.m. walk. A nap would be a boon, but that I'll do without. My cozy snooze isn't possible on a mission. Besides, we're on a time schedule."

Sammie, with laughter in his eyes, headed toward the path.

The woods became less dense, the way less curved, as they trekked further. Open spaces on both sides of the stream were visible. The grasses on the opposite bank were lower and more compact. Bright black eyes like jet buttons observed them from the foliage.

Jal's thoughts went again to the story of Bogie and Ollie. "Sammie, tell me, has everybody in this country been through troubles? Is that the reason they're here?"

"A mix, Jal. Messengers such as Bea and I have certainly had our share of troubles." He gave Bea an impish glance. "Eli, on the other hand, decided to be a chief messenger. In his life of privilege, everyone loved him and serious troubles got a go-by. True, he struggled in making decisions. Nevertheless, his parents were supportive and helped him to realize his dreams.

"Many others opt to live in this country. You're meeting a few of them each day. It doesn't mean that challenges are behind us, Jal. Alas and alack, dragons are to be vanquished until we immigrate to Syntee's homeland.

"You'll soon meet two exceptional messengers of another Guardian, Ethan. Their native country and Syntee's are in close proximity. I referred to His homeland earlier."

"I must say, my head's swimming from all the things you're telling me. I can't get it straight. Now, you keep talking about another country. This one's enough to learn before I add any extras to my jam-packed query cache."

"Let the head reel, only retain the fact of three: the country you left, the country we're now in, and the home country of Syntee. Those particulars are plenty for you,"

"Sammie, I've been thinking…you told me yesterday we could use our troubles to build a strong inner edifice. I want to tell you and Bea a story."

"Tell away, Jal," Bea said. "We'd be honored to hear it."

"I overheard a conversation about the war before Mom and Dad went into the military. Two members of a group meeting in our house were talking. My cousin Uhlin and I had just come in from picking up class assignments at the TAC."

"Whoa," Bea said, "what is the TAC?"

"Sorry, the Teacher's Access Center. It's the administrative center for our district. The TAC assigns a tutor to supervise a group of six to eight students. We rotate our meetings in each other's homes at monthly intervals. At the time, it happened to be in my home. As I said, Uhlin and I came back on Friday afternoon. We went into the kitchen to get a snack before playing a game on the AI." Bea signaled for him to explain.

"The AI is the automatic instrument connected to the TAC. We send and receive our lessons on it. We meet with an administrator to review our weekly assignments at the TAC. Uhlin and I usually play an action game afterward. Anyhow, I glanced into our dining room, and two people were talking. One said, 'We could just surrender.' The other person threw his hands up, waving his arms back and forth, and said, 'Here now, none of that talk. We don't want no straw houses round here.'

"Uhlin and I went to my room to play our game, and I forgot the conversation. It came back when you were talking yesterday. Last night I thought about the words, 'No straw houses round here.'

"Then, I remembered the story Mom read to me when I was four years old. I liked the fabutale of the three pigs who built their own houses. Mom read it to me two or three times a week. Two pigs built their house of straw, and the third one built his of bricks. When the wolf came prowling round, the two straw houses fell down, but the brick one didn't. The wolf wasted his breath and had to slink off. You spoke about recycling hurts into bricks. The story says the same thing. Huh, Sammie?"

"Yes, I'm sure it does, Jal. We must try to take the story's wise advice, to build with enduring materials, in this case bricks. We don't want any wolves prowling round here to have his nose tweaked by you."

"You're a most uncommon boy," Bea said. "You told a good story. Thank you for sharing with us."

She spoke softly to Sammie. "The young'un is sorting out the past and the present, and his draft is well designed."

"You two quit that. Don't talk about me. I'd stomp out of the room when Mom and Dad did it. Nowhere to stomp here, but yelling I can do."

"Enough," Bea replied. "Our maws are sealed. See?" She made a motion of zipping up her lips.

15

The path inclined upward and leveled off, revealing a hillside of diverse green plants in terraced rows. "Fruit," Bea smacked her lips, "umm-umm. Look, Jal, as I said the farm is enormous. All the berries are lip-smacking good! The majority of the fruits are strawberries, blueberries, and blackberries.

"Harvest is past, but these type of berries are special hybrids made to grow later in the year. Ben and Cecil came up with the formula for them. They're extra sweet but not quite ripe yet. At the next gathering, you'll be meeting the sowers and the reapers. Rather soon, I imagine. This home is the ending of many a traveler."

The path became a graveled road with white flowering trees on each side.

Bea pointed and said, "Cherry trees, specially selected for fall blooming."

The graveled road led to a large two-storied house with a terrace and a verandah on the side. Painted a cheerful springtime green, it stood upon an incline sloping downward to the stream. A pathway lined by rose and pink flowers led up to the house. A girl appeared in the doorway and yelled, "Mama, they're here!" Then she jumped off the terrace and sprinted in their direction.

A fair-haired woman called out from the terrace.

"Don't rush so, child."

The girl kept running. Jal slackened his steps and watched as she sped along. Bea and Sammie laughed.

"Ora," Bea said. "She's hardly ever still; a darter and a dasher."

Ora reached them, breathless, and between gasps for air said, "I sat on the terrace all day, Bea and Sammie.

"Are you Jal? We've been on the lookout for you for ever so long."

Breathless and chattering nonstop, she accompanied them while Bea, with her wings fluttering, attempted to insert comments. Jal viewed the gleaming luster of Bea's colors against the darkness of Ora's hair. *Like a spray of flowers*, he thought.

Ollie, waiting on the side verandah, welcomed them warmly. "Eli has been updating us on your journey. Ora have been so excited for two days she can scarcely do her chores."

She ushered them into the kitchen and said, "Jal, meet Ada and Mae. Excitable Ora, the one who is in perpetual motion, needs no introduction."

Jal thought they were the most beautiful girls he had ever seen. He couldn't decide which was the prettiest. Ada had fair hair like her mother, with dark brown eyes. Mae had auburn-colored hair with blue eyes. Ora had dark hair and dark eyes, almost black. *Just like me and Mom,* he thought.

Ada said, "We want your visit to be pleasant, Jal. I'd better postpone my kiss until you leave. No cause for your blushes." She hugged Sammie and kissed Bea.

"You'll get hugs too, Jal," Mae said. "Though I think I'll give you one this minute." She promptly followed up on her statement.

Ollie took charge and suggested that Ora take them to their rooms. "Relax in the quietness, and appreciate your dinner the more. It's tiring being on the trail without respite. Bogie and I are veterans of the road and can attest to that! We'll have the food ready in a little while."

Ora led them upstairs and showed them to a bedroom with a bath. The room was a pleasant blue and white, with a window overlooking the stream. *The stream seems to be everywhere in this country!* Jal said to himself.

"Bea, I have a showoff place for you. Your very own room, next to mine," Ora said.

In the hallway, she opened an exquisite door of carved roses complete with a minute doorknob. "For you, Bea. Mae and I selected the colors and painted it, and the boys did the bathroom. Bo made the door and the bed and Alistair the chest. Mama and Ada sewed the curtains and the spread. Your own room, no more sleeping with me."

Oooh's and aah's spilled from Bea as she went inside the pink-and-cream room. She came out bubbling with excitement. She twirled about the hallway twice. "Thanks so much to everyone."

She stumbled in a twirl and said tactfully. "I'll miss sleeping with you, Ora."

"Yes, me too," Ora replied, "but this is a lot better. You won't get half drowned in our bath from my splattering. These teeny towels are expressly for you; see, I embroidered your name on them. Try them out while I go downstairs and help with dinner."

"Be with you guys in a minute. I'll just scoot inside," Bea said. High-pitched hums and sounds of splashing came from her room. Sammie and Jal, dressed and waiting in the hall for her, chortled in delight.

"Bea is singing," Sammie said.

"More like twittering," Jal responded.

On rejoining the group in the kitchen, Bea said, "A perfect room, thanks to everyone."

"It was so much fun to put together; we should thank you," Ada replied.

"Bogie and the boys will be here within the hour," Ollie said. "And I'm pleased to tell you there is a gathering this evening. We're celebrating recent marriages, births, and our many blessings. This is a holiday weekend for everyone, our third of the year. Porter and his band will be with us, an extra special boost to our party. We'll break up at ten tonight, for you three must be off at morning sunrise."

Mae brought in the drinks and gave one to each. "Pink lemonade, Jal," she said demurely. "It goes well with those brown eyes of yours."

Jal, with eyes averted, took the glass from her without speaking. *I'll ask Sammie how she knew,* he thought.

The opening of the front door interrupted their pleasant half hour of chatter. Two adolescent boys burst into the room. Ollie scolded them. After their boisterous greeting, she sent them upstairs to shower and change clothes. A tall, dark-haired, dark-eyed man with a pleasant smile entered.

"I'm Bogie," he said to Jal and excused himself with a brief hello to Bea and Sammie.

"We'll talk about your journey during dinner; the boys are in their customary state—famished. I'll be back in a minute."

Bea sipped her nectar while the family and Jal ate a roast with potatoes and fresh vegetables. She thanked them for her room and said to Bo and Alistair. "Your handiwork invites a kiss from me.

And here it is. My inexpressible thanks are scarcely adequate for your efforts."

"Your thanks are both eloquent and adequate," Ada replied, to much laughter about the table. "We heard your merry singing. We might even devise another project so Dad and the boys can listen in."

Sammie ate his grains and summed up the particulars of their mission.

"Thank you for sharing with us. We've received news of your journey but only in broad outlines," Bogie said. "We're pleased to have you as a citizen, Jal."

Glass high, Ada said. "I propose a toast; raise your glasses. To Jal and his citizenship."

"I think I'll stay awhile. This country is pretty good," Jal said, and thanked them.

"Lest I forget, Mae has updated news," Ollie said. "Today she made her decision."

"I want to care for the animals instead of doing inside work. I'll do morning studies first and then join our farm manager and Dad in the afternoons," Mae explained to Bea, Sammie, and Jal.

"An ideal job for the animal lover you are, Mae," Alistair said and hugged her.

Bo said, "You quit your dithering, eh?"

"I'll certainly miss you in the house," Ada said. "Who am I going to bicker with over the chores and making pies?" She glanced around the table and said, "No help for it, she'll have to do. So, get ready Ora."

Ora said with a mischievous smile, "I might just stagger you. I listen to you and Mae."

"Indulge in my lemon pie, the last one forever more." Mae said with a frothy browned concoction in her hands.

"Not me," Bea said, shaking her head in refusal. "It might spoil my dainty figure. Sammie likes pie."

"Your dainty figure spoils a go at an epicurean delight," Sammie said.

"I'll have an extra big slice, Mae."

"On my nicest china plate, Sammie."

The after-dinner chores were hastily finished, and everyone scattered to tidy up. Within the hour, the residents filled the large flagstone courtyard at the rear of the house. Jal sat and registered the converging of individuals and groups from different directions. Bea and Sammie moved among the throng, talking and laughing.

Jal spotted Porter and his band arriving with their instruments. They stepped to a podium midway in the courtyard, and Porter opened the show.

How did Porter get here so fast? I'll ask Sammie later. And my other questions too. Jal's thoughts were fleeting as the music absorbed his attention. Porter's bass singer, whom he introduced as Fergie, had a deep, rich voice, prompting loud applause. Bogie and Ollie led in the square dancing, and Ora persuaded Jal to join with her friends in a roundelay.

After the gathering ended, Porter sat and chatted with Jal, Bea, and Sammie. He introduced Fergie to them and said, "I hope to recruit Missy by year's end. A great combination, Fergie's bass and Missy's soprano."

Fergie agreed. "I sneaked a listen to Missy's singing at Callie's insistence. A splendid voice. We can do an operetta at the Christmas pageant."

"We're eager to hear the duet, Fergie," Sammie said. "Perhaps at Eli's next gathering, even before the Christmas one."

"Porter, anytime we listen to your band is a joy," Bea said. "I won't ask how so many activities are packed into your schedule."

"Sammie, we'd better heed Molly's advice and be off upstairs." She motioned to Jal, who bobbed his head in a drowsy, aye.

Reposing in bed, Jal's thoughts reverted to Porter. *How did he make his speedy appearance?*

"Sammie, he can't fly, so how did Porter get here so fast?" he asked.

"I will answer that question. He took a shortcut, Jal. Various routes meander this way, and if you're giving thought to why we haven't taken a shorter one, I'll tell you. Syntee decided it wouldn't do. You'll see why later. Patience, my boy; mysteries are likes seeds planted underground. They grow for a season and then come to harvest. In the proper time, you will reap. Wait for your answer."

"What else can I do except wait, since I don't have a choice? There goes that word choice; I can't seem to get rid of it." Jal groaned. "Goodnight, Sammie."

"Goodnight, dear boy."

Jal reviewed the day's events and found them good. *A terrific day, four days now.* He brought the words of his mother from his memory cache and repeated them to himself until sleep arrived and brought dreams of dark hair and dancing with Ora.

Fifth Day
16

Immersed in a dream of home, Jal heard a far off, insistent voice like a buzzing sound. He opened his eyes, still groggy with sleep, to a blurred figure shaking him. "Time to get up, sleepy head; time to hit the road. Bea's already downstairs eating everything in sight."

"Okay, Sammie, wait for me."

Jal showered and dressed, paying special attention to his hair. He detected a slight smile on Sammie's face as he pulled on his shoes. They went downstairs and joined the group in the dining room. During breakfast, the family chatted about activities for the evening. Ada and Mae suggested a booth on the lawn for desserts.

Ora said, "I'll have a popcorn table. I wish you could stay, Jal. I make a best-seller popcorn."

"More tables and chairs might be a good idea since you girls are adding refreshments," Bogie said. "Let's go, boys, before you're inveigled into making pies." They said good-bye and left to do the setting up.

"Please, excuse me," Ollie interrupted the chatter. "Sammie, lunches are packed. Don't forget them, and enjoy the tidbits. I hope you like yours, Jal."

"Thanks," Sammie replied. "Bea would never let me forget. Your lunches are first class."

Bea expressed regret at having to miss the rest of the gathering.

"The next one," Ollie said, "and you too, Jal."

"Now for that hug," Ada said, giving Jal a kiss.

"Me too, another for me," Mae said.

"Don't forget me," Ora said.

Jal, blushing, stoically permitted the kisses.

Affectionate good-byes were exchanged, and they got underway by fits and starts. Sammie promptly forgot his rucksack with their lunch inside. After enduring a scolding from Bea, he retrieved it to another round of sendoffs.

Jal took a deep breath of the early-morning air, sweet and fresh. In the thin light from the open door, the dewdrops fell from the flowers like bits of glass.

As they reached the path, he glanced upwards at a half moon and a bright star.

"Downright great, Sammie, Bea, look!"

"If I stretch, maybe I can touch them," Bea said and raised on her tiptoes. "Nope, my fingers won't reach that far. You'll just have to grow taller, Sammie."

"Not likely, Bea."

"That's the morning star, Jal. We think it's marvelous too," she said.

"This evening, you'll meet Mel and Cal. They're joining us for dinner at the guesthouse," Sammie said. "Mel and Cal are warrior messengers of Ethan, the Guardian of the East. Our eager ears expect a clue-in on their latest mission. Ordinarily, Syntee reveals the details of their doings to us. For some reason, though, He and Ethan sent them in person today. Bea and I consider it an honor to be their friends. So will you, Jal."

"Warriors? What does a warrior messenger mean, Sammie?"

"Just wait until you meet them."

"Now, how did you learn about Mel and Cal being at the guesthouse, Sammie? How did you find out? You were with me yesterday and last night," Jal said, while he eyed Sammie. "And how did Bea know there would be a gathering last night?"

"Wait a little while, and I promise to explain."

Jal squeezed his eyes tightly closed, opened his mouth, and exhaled. "Okay, Sammie, I guess I can wait. I must say, I'm learning to wait in double time; I do it so much. The two of you say that more than Mom. 'No, Jal, you have to wait. You're too young,' she says when I ask for things on her veto manual. My vetoed list is growing into a series!"

Sammie grinned without replying.

Bea, balanced on Sammie's head, cut in. "I'll tell you Molly's story if you wish."

Jal focused his eyes on her lustrous changing colors. Her cheery words diverted his thoughts. "I'd like for you to tell me. I've been thinking about Molly and Callie. How did they get to Eli's home? We'll listen to the birds and animals before you tell me their stories."

"My thoughts exactly. We'll get to the guesthouse in early evening. We can walk slower if you wish."

Jal nodded his head. "Yes, we'll sit longer at lunch and practice forgetting the 'we can walk slower' speech from your pampered podium."

Bea tapped him sharply on the head, resumed her seat, and said, "My pampered place indeedy!"

"I like to see you sitting on Sammie's head. Your colors are like my whirligig spinning at high speed."

"Now I'm a fount of entertainment! I'll add that to my bagatelle of amusements. And later you can tell me what a whirligig is," she replied.

Sammie and Jal laughed. The early-morning sun scattered tints of pale gold and a blush of pink on the path before them.

The stream in a lilting monotone differed from its ordinary rising and falling.

"No song for us. I guess it's taking a break," Jal said.

"What?" Bea said.

"The stream," Jal replied.

Distant rustlings of the woodland creatures were the only indication of their presence. "They seem to be working farther away today," Sammie said.

"I'm ready to tell my story now." Bea said, interrupting their musings.

Jal wrinkled his nose at her. "Ho-hum, should we let her, Sammie?"

"She does seem determined, Jal."

"You two are the most aggravating things; I'm going to tell Syntee on you both," she said with a frown, rapping them on their heads.

"Please, don't tell Syntee." Sammie folded his hands in a pleading gesture. He grinned at Jal, who folded his hands and repeated Sammie's words.

She rapped them on their heads again. "I know what you two are. You're termagants. Go figure that out! One day I was fussing and Syntee said to me. 'You must struggle against becoming a termagant, Bea.' No, wait! You can go figure after I tell my story. Be sure to notify me when you do. I have no inkling of its meaning."

"Okay, your story—we'll forget about figuring things out, perhaps permanently," Sammie replied in a placid tone. "Including telling Syntee."

"We'll forget it. I'm too rash, Syntee tells me I am."

She stroked Jal's hair. "My story begins like this. Molly lived with her mom on a farm in a Southern country bordering yours. Your former one, that is."

"Has everyone we met lived on a farm?" Jal asked.

"You're chiefly meeting farm inhabitants because Syntee chose the path most appropriate for you," Sammie said. "I think we talked about it a day or two ago. There are other paths leading to cities. Bea and I traveled to a city on one occasion. What a mess! Syntee said to us when we got home, 'No more urban tours for you two. Country routes will do.'"

Bea broke in, "The centerpiece is Molly's story, and we'll tell you our city adventure another time. Heaps of yarns are in store for you."

"You and Sammie have mentioned the Nitecraulers, and now a city tale. Why won't you let me in on the know?"

"The stories we've selected relate to those you're meeting, Jal. Our own personal escapades are not so relevant. Get familiar with Grandfather Moutyn and his village. Then we'll come clean on the Nitecrauler rumpus. Two rows of unspeakable beings converged on us, chanting, 'I'll grind you to a nubbin and feed you to the pigs.' With each chant they stopped, stomped their feet, and roared. Their roar boosted a pitch higher the closer they came to us.

"We endured six hours of horror—a century to us. Our disobedience didn't stop Syntee from sending Mel and Cal to our rescue. We were so thankful for our bailout that we groveled in the dust for weeks. Sorry penitents, the both of us. Moreover, we endured hearing loss for months afterwards."

"Sounds like a stupendous adventure. Another wait, is it? I'm getting used to the word *waiting*, so on with Molly's story, please, Bea."

"Molly grew up on the farm, as I said. She and her mom, Emmie, led a sheltered life, with little disturbance in their pacific days—that is, until Molly became an adolescent. One afternoon she and a friend went to a neighbor's birthday party. Caught up in the festivities, they were late in getting home. Molly, expecting a severe scolding, loitered outside. At sundown, she waited for a summons to dinner. *She must be furious*, Molly said to herself, after an hour's wait.

"Worried, and hungry, she went inside. To her dismay, the house was silent and empty, and not a sign of dinner preparations. The absence of her mom shook her to such an extent that she became panic-stricken. She rushed from one neighbor to another. No one knew her whereabouts. Molly, hysterical by this time, expanded her search to the outlying area. Late at night, she regained enough self-control to realize she was lost.

She crawled under some shrubs moaning with terror, and near morning, she fell into a troubled sleep.

"Eli, on his way home from a mission, heard sounds of whimpering. He explored and found Molly asleep in the underbrush. Unwilling to awaken her in the darkness, he waited for the sunrise. At daybreak, Molly stirred and poked her head out. On seeing Eli, she began screaming. He spoke to her in soothing tones and calmed her down sufficiently to answer his questions. She had no idea of how to get home. After a great deal of coaxing, she consented to go home with Eli. Comforted by his promise to search for her mother, she accepted the care of Porter and his family.

"Emmie arrived within a week. She explained her absence to Molly. 'Just after you and Lia left, Mrs. Odem came to the door; she was ill and needed medical attention. I took her to the health clinic and stayed until the doctor arrived. I must have been with her four hours or more. After the doctor's examination, he sent her to the hospital. I had no way of letting you know that afternoon...it was such a mix-up. How worried I've been! I thought I would be back long before you came in. The urgency of the situation demanded my attention, and I forgot to leave a note for you Molly.'

"They conferred with Eli and decided to make their citizenship status permanent. They share a small cottage near Porter's family. Luellen and her mom taught Molly home management skills and culinary arts. She advanced rapidly and officially assumed her domestic duties within two years. Three aides help in the assorted tasks of household maintenance. Callie is her assistant in the kitchen area. Mollie says her happiness is right at home.

"'Traveling is not for me,' she says to us.

"But traveling is for Sammie and me, Jal. Any questions?"

"No, no questions, but what a happy ending. I hope mine will end like hers. About Molly, she seems so cheerful. It's hard to imagine her lost in the woods. Batches of sad tales! I love them. They are sad, a lot of them, but the ending is happy. I love the wrap-ups."

17

The trees were thinning out, and multiple folds of blue hills blended into the far vista. The stream fell in miniature waterfalls that seemed to reflect the blue of the hills. An assortment of creatures, plentiful now, peeped at them from the undergrowth below the trees.

"Sammie, do you think they like us?" Jal asked, pointing to the peeping eyes.

"I suspect they do, when we like them. They have a place of their own, as we do, and are cautious about extending invitations to their homes."

In the stillness, Jal walked and thought of the creatures that lived in the woods.

They sat on a bank by the stream and ate their lunch. Jal's paper bag contained a sandwich, soup, fruit, and a chocolate drink.

"My nectar," Bea said. "You want to know why I drink it every single meal. I just do. The summer drought scarcity? Whatever the cause, the varieties are more than enough for me."

"My grains too, and without a drought to fault for liking them," Sammie said.

"A feast for the least. Don't muzzle my guzzle. Hey Sammie, I made two rhymes. The flowers grow on Bogie's farm, and Porter mixes the nectars. A winning match up."

"I don't eat the same thing, but I wouldn't mind. The food is lip-smacking scrummy, and the conversation is superb," Jal commented.

"The superb goodies for you two, and a mix of roasted nuts for me." Sammie said, handing them each a portion

"My favorite," Bea said and took her pink nectar.

"Aaa-ha, I thought you said you liked Eli's best."

"Oh, you, Jal! Yes I do, ordinarily." Bea crinkled her eyes at him and moved them from side to side. "But this pink nectar is um-um tasty. Can't I like both equally?"

"I guess so," he replied, laughing. "I say the same thing. This berry cobbler is plumb unbeatable."

"The whirligig you referred to," Bea said. "What is it?"

"A parti-colored paper wheel pinned to a wooden rod and wound up by a key. It whirled and cast shimmering colors on the walls and ceiling of my room at night. Mom's gift to me when she was home on leave."

"Sorry, the pretty has absconded."

"Me too. I'm a little old for it anyway. I'm past the toy stage. What's more, I feel like I am." Jal gave a rueful shrug, took his shoes and socks off, and dabbled his feet in the shallow water.

The sun glinted in stippled patterns of light and dark on the stream. The fronds of the grasses moved in the soft breeze, as if waving a greeting to them. The elusive golden shadow passed, and Jal watched without comment. Then he altered his position and considered Sammie, who sat placidly eating nearby. *I do so want to be like Sammie*, he said to himself.

A gust of wind ruffled Jal's hair as they stepped on the path. *Like Mom's touch*. Preoccupied by his thoughts of home, he didn't hear Sammie until Bea tapped on his head.

"Mel and Cal are the messengers of Ethan we mentioned. We met them when they rescued us from the Nitecraulers. " Sammie said. " In the following year, we participated in a mission with them. We suspect Syntee wished to assure us of His trust. Our willful behavior had kept us in the clutch of the doldrums for months."

"They also do investigative work as private detectives. Whenever the process of justice fails, they probe into the incidents, Mel said. The offenses range from major to minor, including criminal ones. They gather proofs and examine the facts pertaining to the case under investigation. Their findings and evidence are then passed on to the proper authorities for judicial purposes.

"Bea and I aren't in the loop of their detective service. Their work isn't here; it may be...aw...forget it. I'm not quite clear on the whereabouts of their detectings and investigatings. Their home country and Syntee's are in the same constellation. They did tell us that. Someday I intend to ask them to share some of their case notes with us."

Jal stood motionless. Sammie and Bea's extra-special roles had entered his awareness for the first time. "You do missions— I mean more valiant ones than with me? I learned that word by reading Prince Valiant in the comics. Mom gave me four volumes with an RI when I was five years old. Valiant sounds like my name Valhyn, doesn't it?"

"Exactly right for the names of two champs," Bea said. "Pray tell, what is an RI?"

"We use the device in learning to read, and in our studies; it's a gadget that projects words onto a blank page. I lost the Tot so often Mom attached it to my pocket with a lock. She'd take my chips to pay for the replacement. 'Straitened funds for you next month, Jal,' she'd say. I left it in my room the night I slept under the willow tree."

"Okay, Bea, don't say a word. Tot means tools of the trade."

"We have Tots, and we'll enlarge your store of info with the details anon." Bea said.

"I won't reply to that statement," Jal said. "I know your answer."

"Sammie, about your valiant missions? Enough of the RI and the Tot."

"We do go on other missions, Jal, whenever Syntee gives us assignments, but more valiant ones than this one? I don't know. Indeed, I don't," Sammie said, grinning. "Your attention evidently strayed while we were telling you our stories, distracted, no doubt, by other matters. Bea and I classify you as a meditative sort of fellow."

"I do like to think about the things you tell me. You too, Bea. I'm so fascinated by your stories. You don't expect me to remember everything, do you?"

"Certainly not. Bea and I were on a few scary adventures in the past. Generally, the missions are safe; we've had minimal risky incidents. The one with Mel and Cal—we'll add the account to your queued ones. Their world is a mystery to us that we intend to unravel. Possibly we three can do the unraveling together. They are singular beings. When you meet them... you'll agree with us."

"We'll tell you Porter's story instead," Bea added. "Please, Sammie, will you tell him?" she asked, fluttering in front of him with beseeching eyes.

"Okay, I can't refuse, can I? You'd be a chronic grouser. I love Porter's story, and Bea does too. She prefers the listening to the telling part."

"Please, Sammie, maybe you can begin his story, since we'll get to the guesthouse early. I do like Porter, almost as much as Uhlin."

"You respond to Porter just like Bea and I did on our introduction to him. He's rather a legend in this country. And you are a boy for a legend. A little farther on, I'll begin."

"I can't wait for Uncle Joulh to meet Porter and Eli. He's sort of adventurous like them."

"Adventurous, huh? Must be a family trait. Eh, Bea?"

"I fear so, Sammie."

Jal gave them a dubious look. "You mean me."

"Time to shift this conversation," Sammie replied. "Are you ready?"

"For Porter's story, I am."

18

"The enchantment of Porter's story remains fresh for me as well as Bea," Sammic said. "He's the oldest of eight, and his given name is Porter Andrew. He was the odd one of the family; still is, in fact. When he was seven years old, he asked his mom, Seraphina, for a violin. She, being a loving and wise mother, said she would help him buy one. Porter ran errands for the neighboring farmer to earn money. His brothers and sisters contributed, and soon, by his eighth birthday, the violin was his.

"Porter applied himself to his goal of becoming an excellent player. Years went on, and his violin skills grew, though never to the neglect of his farm duties. He carried on his work as a devoted son, but for years, he harbored a secret longing. He dreamed of becoming a great musician in a city band. At eighteen years of age, the yearning intensified. Sometimes while doing a task, he would pause, as if he were seeing some inner drama on a private screen.

"His mom kept tabs on his aberrant behavior, so unlike his brothers and sisters. Several months went by. Then at a closing of a weekly family meeting, she detained him for a few minutes. She asked for an explanation of his unusual behavior. Porter blurted out his secret desire to be a musician in a city band. 'Mama, I feel like I'm a bad son for wishing to leave the family, but my heart is so heavy with this longing.'

"She listened to him, nonplussed but thoughtfully. 'Let me sleep on this, Porter. I'll think on what you've said and give you an answer tomorrow.'

"Porter and his mom were up before the others on most mornings, and this morning was no exception. She brewed coffee, filled two cups, and then said, 'Porter, let's sit down and discuss these longings in your heart.'

"'The dream is at the forefront of my every waking hour, Mama. It's been eight years, and I can't seem to shake it off. Am I a bad son for being so obsessed with my music? Please tell me, Mama.'

"'Porter, if your longings are so strong, you need to pursue your dreams. As you grow older, you would blame me for your unrealized musical ambitions. You are a good son to me, and whether you're here or someplace else won't change that fact. We'll schedule a family discussion this evening, if it's okay with you.'

"'Sure, Mama.' Porter said, embracing her.

"To the multiple why questions for the meeting, Mama replied, 'You will learn this evening.' The family members could hardly wait to assemble after dinner.

"The instant Porter announced his plans, the younger ones began crying. The older ones gaped at him in amazement. Mama spoke to them in a resolute tone.

"'Porter's plans are definite; He has an opportunity to perform with a topnotch band of musicians. When his success is evident, he will join an international band.'

"His brothers and sisters gawped at Porter, speechless, for a long minute. Then, everyone jumped up and began talking at the same time.

"Mama calmed them down and said, 'Luellan, you're qualified to take charge of Porter's responsibilities. You're more than ready from your training this year. He can be free to leave in a couple of weeks.'

"Luellen said, 'Indeed, Mama, I can handle Porter's job. I do the household accounts now.

"'You're a sly one Porter. So that's the reason you wanted me to learn your job.'

"Porter gave her a contrite glance without replying.

"'Surely, each of the family members can manage a few more odd jobs,' Porter's mom said and ended the meeting. She waited for their answers. Minutes went by; then, thunderstruck still, everyone agreed to take on the extra chores.

"Porter prepared to leave with a lightened heart after gaining his family's support. He promised to visit often and to play his violin for family gatherings. Everyone hid their sadness and remained cheerful until he had left to join his musician friends.

"Porter and the band gained fame within a year. Both critics and audiences praised his musical skills. In six months, they were traveling cross-country, and a year later they were touring the UK and the Continent. He had secured entrance to the best international band: his current one. On the other hand, he found it impossible to keep his promise for frequent family visits.

"His fame grew, and he told himself he was overjoyed with his star status, and so he was for a year or more. He valued the friendship of his fellow musicians and his continental travels. Still, dreams of family and the happy times he had known on the farm filled his sleeping hours. His present successful life never entered into his dreams, which baffled him. *'I have reached my goals. Why do these tiresome dreams persist?'* He asked himself.

"He constantly told himself he lived a celebrated life. Wherever the band went, someone in the audience would exclaim, 'Hey isn't that a P...in the band?' or 'That P...can really play the fiddle!' If they were in a ritzy place with a trendy audience, someone would say, 'Isn't it marvelous that a P...a brilliant violinist, isn't he?' He brushed aside the remarks, and when the band members teased him, he laughed it off.

"Porter fell in love with a renowned actor, Maria Selena, a.k.a., MsPikee, while on a tour in England. The subject of marriage came up. Porter hesitated to make a commitment because she moved in modish social groups. His simple tastes fitted in poorly with her fashionable friends. He waffled for a year or more, indecisive and uncertain. She, tiring of his evasions, rendered the decision moot. On a six-month continental tour with her acting troupe, she met a prominent banker in Berlin, Germany. They were married within six weeks. Porter was devastated for a month or two but soon mended without any notable effects.

"Over the five years that Porter performed on the world's stage, he acquired fame and money galore. His music kept him continually on the go. He only managed three visits home during his incessant travels. He told himself daily he was happy. His family conveyed their pride in him in each of the long letters he received weekly.

"He had learned to shrug off his occasional dreams. To his vexation, however, they escalated to a nightly routine. His music took a nosedive. One afternoon he missed band practice, and then it became a regular occurrence. It was unlike Porter; he was dependable and punctilious in the practice sessions. For a spell, he muddled through his nightly acts. However, within a month he missed a rehearsal and two nights' engagements. A week later, he muffed another one. This time the bandleader sent a doctor to examine him.

"After the doctor's examination, he said, 'Porter you are ill from exhaustion and depression. In order to regain your health I advise you to take an extended rest.'

"The doctor recommended a private retreat on the seashore. Porter took his counsel. He packed up, said good-bye to the band members, and moved to a cottage by the sea.

"He took long walks every day along the seacoast; his dreams of family were less frequent as he regained his health and could think more rationally. One morning, from nowhere, the thought came to mind, *I have achieved my longed-for goals and even much more. But where was I the happiest? With my mom, brothers and sisters. The peace I knew on the farm is lost. What have I gained? Perhaps it's time for other aims.* His thoughts circled about in his head, 'Like incessant flea bites,' he said when describing them to Eli. His walks became a little longer each day as he pondered his past and his future.

"When he began to roam farther from the seashore, he carried an overnight backpack with him. One evening, he found himself deep in a forest, miles from his cottage by the sea. He spread his sleeping bag below a big tree.

"Eli, on his way home from a mission, spied Porter and spoke to him in passing. He spent the night in the area, and the next morning, he went by and invited Porter to breakfast. Porter observed Eli, so big and golden, and for an instant felt a touch of fear. He gazed into Eli's eyes, sensed his gentleness and kindness, and without hesitation accepted his invitation. They shared a repast from Eli's provisions then and there under the tree.

"Eli had matters to attend to in another part of the region, but he and Porter agreed to meet the next afternoon at the seashore. A lasting friendship stemmed from their meeting that day.

"Eli shared with him a portion of his own life story and a condensed account of his work."

Jal cut in, "Porter had the same reaction I did when I first met Eli, didn't he?"

"So he did," Sammie replied.

"Look at me," Bea said. "I'm a minuscule being, but I was never afraid of Eli."

"Heh! Because you knew he couldn't see you. You're so small," Jal said.

"You...you're a rascally urchin, you are."

"Sammie, take up your tale and forbid this child to talk."

"Maybe I'd better. Go on, that is," Sammie replied.

"Porter spoke to Eli of his confused emotional state in a nonstop chatting session. And it seemed as if he were in a debate with himself. After their visit, it became clear to Porter that his old ambitions were no longer relevant. His wish for fame and money had gone—but what to do with his life?

"One evening, he mentioned his mixed-up state of mind to Eli, who offered little advice. Instead, he extended an invitation. 'Porter, put the matter aside and come for a relaxing visit to my home. You may see things in a different perspective on review.'

"He accepted Eli's invitation for a weekend, which he extended to a week. Molly, Callie, and Montague liked him right off. Monty designated himself the tour guide and each day took him off to visit one of the farm's projects. In the evenings, Porter entertained them with his violin. 'I haven't had so much fun since leaving home,' he said to Eli at the end of his visit.

"He went back to his seaside cabin with a more decisive mindset. *My life as a musician is over*, he said to himself. *I know that I was happiest in useful family activities. I'll ask Eli for his opinion and then try for a definite decision.'*

"Porter discussed his thoughts with Eli a day later. 'My mind is still somewhat burdened with the fear of making another decision I might regret later. I would be most grateful for any guidance you can give me. What do you consider my best move to be? Is the family farm to be my life's work?'

"Eli regarded Porter with solicitous eyes before replying. 'Decisions once made are acts that we live with Porter; few are so set in stone that we can't reverse or revisit them. Disregard any fears about decision-making. We can only know the immediate present and proceed from the moment. But let me tell you of another opportunity.' He spoke to him of his need for a business manager and asked him to consider the position.

"'It's a service even greater than the family farm. Enlarge your reach, Porter. What is more, I want someone who thoroughly knows the farming trade. Your skills will be utilized to their utmost, and you would be a significant support in my missions.'

"'Eli,' Porter said, 'you have helped me so much. No words can express how thankful I am to you, and now you offer me a job in your noble endeavors I can say yes right now. From the day of our meeting, I've admired your work. Part of me has dared to hope that I might share in the enterprise. Even though you might think my answer is too soon, it sounds so right to me. I'll gladly accept and serve faithfully in whatever capacity you think suitable. I will ask you, however, for a favor. I want to invite my mother, brothers, and sisters to come live on your farm.'

"'Of course, you may. They would be a fine addition to our community.'

"'I'll be at your door within a month, either alone or with my family. There's quite a troop of us, Eli.'

"And thus, he made his decision. Porter folded up his tent and located his band. After a brief summary of his healing at the seashore, he informed them of his decision to become Eli's business manager. He asked them to make a habit of visits to the farm. The bandleader expressed his regret at losing Porter, but everyone promised a stopover between gigs.

"Porter went home to his family, who was jubilant at his homecoming. They listened spellbound as he described his life in the musical world. He gave them an account of his illness and his meeting with Eli. He shared the specifics of his emotional turmoil at the seashore and disclosed his intent to become Eli's farm manager. His family, confounded yet again, listened in wordless absorption to his story.

"'Porter,' Luellen said, 'we thought you couldn't stun us anymore, but this one beats all!'

"'Wait till you hear this then!' he said to them. 'I want everyone to move with me to Eli's farm. He's a great being; one senses that it is so in his presence. And he willingly offers us a home and work suitable to our skills. The decision to stay or go is yours; don't think I'm coercing you. Persuading? Yes, I am.'

"He discussed details of Eli's work with them in two family meetings. 'It's a tremendous opportunity, dear ones. I don't want to be separated from you ever again.'

"The family was impressed with Porter's report of Eli's work and met in private to discuss the possibility of relocating. 'It's quirky and sudden, but that's just like Porter,' Luellen said. She and Mercy Vine decided to go for a week's stay. A final decision depended on the report they brought back.

"Porter contacted Eli, and in three days, Luellen and Mercy Vine were off for the visit. Both sisters came home enthused. They gave their report in a private family session excluding Porter. 'You might influence our decision,' Mercy Vine said.

"Porter's brothers sallied out of the meeting exclaiming, 'Groovy adventure, and ready to go!'

"Alifair and Malinda, engaged to the sons of a neighboring farmer, decided on marriage before the family's move.

"'We'll stay here, Mama, Alifair and I,' Malinda said. 'William and Meredith's father needs them on the farm. Perhaps later, we can join you.' The future sisters-in-law assisted with the bridal arrangements and within two weeks became supporting actors in a double wedding.

"The neighboring farmer bought their homestead as a wedding gift to his sons. 'Family matters,' he said to Seraphina. The packing and the mundane matters of moving the family's belongings were finished off. In a trice, Porter and his mother, Winston, Peregrine, John William, Luellen, and Mercy Vine were on their way to Eli's farm.

"'Even before the month is up,' Porter said to himself.

"Porter's tenth year with Eli is past. He and his family are content contributors to the community. He has never regretted or questioned his decision. His two sisters live at the old home place and bring their families on a yearly visit. On leaving they yet say, 'Later we can be together, Mama.'

"His mom, Seraphina, is teaching, and caring for new arrivals. Luellen is in charge of Eli's financial and secretarial affairs. His brothers, married now with families of their own, work on the farm. Mercy Vine wed a young man, a long-term resident, two years after her arrival."

"What a marvelous whopper of a story. Thank you, Sammie."

"You echo me, Jal," Bea said. "Porter's tale is a masterpiece that reveals new details each time I hear it."

"Does Porter know Grandfather Moutyn?"

Sammie laughed and replied, "Yes, Jal, everyone is well known in this country. Three annual get-togethers at each of the farms and two combined assemblies for all guarantee it. We attend when our work permits and have a cracking good time. Porter formed a band a year or so after settling in.

"In fact, his former musical chums dribble in piece-meal and decide to stay. The bandleader is the latest. They play at the get-togethers and all over the country. The next collective gathering will take place in about a month at Eli's place. Grandfather Moutyn, and the villagers, and you too, will be there."

19

Jal walked, engrossed in thought. The image of his parents and his uncle came into clear focus. Then the figure of Eli superimposed itself on their image. Somehow certainty had taken root and grown within him; he would see them in the not-too-distant future. *It would be great to have them at the gatherings. I'll tell them Porter's story.* On the far side of the stream, the tall grasses stirred in the breeze. *Eli went to Mom, Dad, and Uncle Joulh.* He felt comforted by the thought.

The creatures of the woods were less noisy, the path less curved. Through the leaves, the cloudless sky appeared a cerulean blue. Jal inspected the scintillating particles of sunlight lacing the shadows on the path. He let go of his thoughts.

"Sammie, I do like Porter. Do you think he might allow me to play in his band when I'm old enough? I've had lessons on the saxophone for a couple of years."

"I'd suggest a talk with your mom and dad is in order, Jal. You may discover things that are more exciting. Put music on hold for a year or two, and then reassess. Trial and error can be a fine teacher.

"Okay, Sammie. If you think it best. On ice it is. Reminds me, Ceil was on ice too, eh?"

Bea added, "I guess he was at that, mine own jester. Good advice from Sammie. I recommend dips in the fount of learning. Mind your saxophone blowing, and reopen the topic. Ahh—here we are at the guesthouse."

A descent in the path coiled round to a shingled cabin set on top of an elevated bank ten or twelve feet from the stream. Two men in formfitting golden-brown suits stood conversing near the porch steps. Dark gold helmets fitted closely to their heads, and knee-high boots of the same gold color encased their lower legs. Each had a sword at his side that glinted in the rays of the setting sun as they advanced to greet them.

"Mel, Cal!" Bea exclaimed. "What a tribute to lowly laborers in the field."

Sammie walked faster and grasped their hands.

Jal, rooted to the spot, examined them.

"Greetings, Jal, I am Cal. You are a charming addition to our country." His copper-colored face melded into his clothes.

Like the antique pictures I've seen in old history books, Jal said to himself.

Cal opened the cabin door and led them inside. "We are to meet with Ethan this evening and must be off by twilight's close. At present, let us eat and rejoice together in the news we bring."

Jal stepped into the room without speaking, his eyes glued to their faces. *Their faces are glowing, and their eyes are the color of the stream,* he thought.

A stew, salad, and a charlotte russe sat on the table with fruit drinks in mugs. A loaf of crusty bread lay in a basket.

"For you, Jal," Mel said and conducted him to a seat. He set Bea's nectar and Sammie's multi-grains in place and sat down.

Sammie and Bea related the details of their present assignment during the meal. Cal then relayed the news of their latest mission. Jal, transfixed by the narrative they recited, kept track of every word in rapt admiration.

"The Nyevyns have regained their homeland," Cal said. "The Worlings are in exile."

On seeing Jal's inquiring eyes, he explained, "The Worlings are an aggressive people from the far north. They sidled into the Nyevyns' villages under a pretext of wanting to learn their peaceful ways. Instead, they loosed a shocking attack that the Nyevyns were unable to resist. At Anthelia's request, Ethan sent us to support her warriors in ousting the Worlings."

"Anthiela, a.k.a., Ann, is the Guardian of the West," Mel said in response to Jal's question. "Cal and I are assigned to Ethan. When required, however, we may unite with the warriors of the three other Guardians. An entrée into our work is

161

pending for you, Jal. The first task is to learn the principles of your present country."

Cal waited until Mel finished. "The Worlings will be in exile until they waive militant ambitions and acquire respect for their neighbors," he said, ending the story.

Sammie urged them to disclose more specifics of their mission after dinner. They stayed until the dimming light indicated the approach of darkness.

Cal stood up. "This stint of sharing has been good, but we must fly, my friends. We don't want to be late for our appointment with Ethan."

"A tryst for us at the hangout, partners. Don't forget," Mel said to Bea and Sammie.

"And you, Jal—we will meet again."

Jal stood in the doorway and kept them under scrutiny as they strode away. To his amazement, they suddenly disappeared. *They moved into the darkness.* He stashed the thought in his query cache. *Answer on hold.*

Jal marched over to Sammie, who was washing and drying the dishes. "Please tell me, is Syntee in charge of warriors?"

"Yes, he is," Sammie replied, "when events require a remedy. Furthermore, Syntee and Ethan combine forces if a deceptive circumstance warrants it. The peace-loving Nyeveyns long ago forgot how to wage war. Syntee says they're an example to each generation and serve as a symbol of hope to the world. 'Someday, wars will be wiped out.' Syntee said when we quizzed Him. Scarcely a week ago, we posed the question, and that is what He told us."

"Oh, how I long for the war to be over. Mom and Dad could be with me for good and Uncle Joulh too!"

"Have faith, Jal," Bea said. "Syntee said you'd be together in a little while. Your mom and dad knew your whereabouts by late morning on the day we left. Why, even now a letter might be in the post for you. In any case, your future with your family is certain, so be of good courage, Jal."

A minute or two went by before he spoke. "Yes, I'll do as Syntee says. I can wait. You and Sammie are my friends."

"Absolutely, we are. We'll see each other often."

"Tell me, Sammie," Jal said with a furrowed brow. "Mel and Cal are warriors. Why don't they stop the war?"

"Now, that's a good question," Sammie replied. "I'll answer it as best I can. Your former country and the other countries of the world are on probation, you might say. We have no idea how long the probation will last. No one knows, not even Syntee, who instructed us in these particulars.

"We do understand it ends when the Owner, the Great High King, reappears. He will take charge and put the kibosh on wars. Cal and Mel will have starring roles in the event. We're to watch and wait for His return. When it will be is a hanging question mark—somewhat like those 'waits and sees' you get from us.

"Meanwhile, the King has appointed Syntee to recruit a workforce for His kingdom, otherwise known as the illustrious country you're currently in, Jal. The four Guardians authorize their messengers to bring in the willing émigrés. We'll understand why the Owner King is patient with the nations of the world as we grow and mature, Syntee says.

"We're slow learners. Maturity hasn't enlightened us, so far. Bea and I admit to a lack of answers for some question that you may ask, Jal. We, too, wait."

"Thank you, Sammie," Jal replied. "I guess I'll wait, like you say...Meantime, you can tell me the King's story. Why didn't you mention Him earlier? You said you wait too?"

"Yes, we do, Jal. Patience, you'll have a series of classes on Him—Bea's number-one hero. A dip is in order and then to bed. An early start in the morning is on the agenda."

"Early it is, Sammie. And a query shredded on who is Bea's number-one hero. Off we go." He hastily changed into his trunks, grabbed his towel and ran to the stream.

Bea zoomed ahead of them. "Hey, I beat you here; this is a good place. Fits me perfectly." She slid into a diminutive pool.

"Don't get your hair wet," Jal said.

"A jokester, eh? Mind your manners, Jal Valhyn," she snapped.

"I suggest you two stage a comedy duo at the next gathering," Sammie said.

Bea wriggled her nose at him and gave a blissful sigh as she dived deeper into the water.

"I owe you bunches, Sammie, and you too, Bea," Jal said, jumping into the stream. "I'm glad I met Mel and Cal. I'm piling up things for my thinking basket—one thing actually. When you were telling me Eli's story, you said Porter contacted Eli. How did he do that, Sammie?"

"The tele-coms went missing; only the military has them. You have no tele-com, or I haven't seen one. I got two letters from Mom, but you didn't get any that I know about. How did you find out that Mel and Cal would be at the cabin? Come to think about it, how do you know Mom and Dad and Uncle Joulh got the news I'm safe?"

Sammie slid deeper into the water and replied, "Another thing to wait on, Jal. I'll explain later."

Bea flipped water at them. "So much waiting. Never mind, Jal."

Jal pretended to scowl. "Okay, Bea, I won't grouse this time, but don't count on doing a bunk because I'm not squawking. Right now, I won't throw water at your hair, or the hair you tell me you have."

"You bold young'un, if this pool weren't so delightful, I'd rap your head," she said testily.

"Sammie, you deal with him."

"Yes, Bea, I will," Sammie replied and plunged under the water.

The water was cool and soothing to tired minds and bodies. The day's journey and the stimulating conversation with Mel and Cal receded into the background. They relaxed in the pool as the still night enfolded them in its serenity. They dried themselves off, went into the cabin, and fell into bed. Jal descended swiftly into a deep slumber filled by dreams of warriors and the rescue of Ora from the Worlings.

Sixth Day
20

Jal awoke to the twittering of the birds outside the open windows. Sammie emerged from the bathroom, rubbing his hair with a towel. Bea was humming a low tune while sampling her nectar.

"Another bright day, Sammie, and the young'un gets to hear my chirpy purring," she said.

Chirpy is the right word. Her singing is more like a bird twitter than a purring, Jal thought as he lay in relaxed comfort, observing their activities.

He got up without saying good morning, showered, and dressed. He sat down and banged his fist on the table. "I want my breakfast, woman," he said to Bea in a loud voice.

"How about that, Sammie? The young'un's getting spunky."

"I'm only teasing, Bea. I can make you breakfast if you'd like. I whipped up an omelet for Mom when she was home on leave."

"An option I'll risk. Maybe tomorrow morning or the next."

Jal savored his multi-grain cereal with milk. Orange juice and a white butter spread on a thick piece of homemade bread drew umm-umms from him.

"A whip-up from yogurt, a Callie special, if I may borrow your words," Bea said. "I mean the butter. It's so good. She makes the butter by hand and bakes the breads. Ollie does luscious jam tarts every week, and they exchange. And you shall have a sample jam tart for lunch."

Sammie fastened the door of the tidy cabin, leaving a note of thanks for the generous offerings.

"Our schedule is off, but the sleep did us good. We've been walking from daylight to dark. A leisurely pace will do for today. We'll reach your new home sometime in the afternoon tomorrow, Jal.

"To change the subject, A desolate section of countryside enlivens our traipse today. You may find the region dismal and a tad creepy. However, Bea and I have been over the area several times. It's a riddle for a boy who thinks."

In response to Jal's inquiring eyes, Sammie said, "A test for a valiant Valhyn."

Jal let go of his questions and focused on his surroundings. *I'll ask Sammie to explain when we get through the creepiness.* The path curled near the stream into an upward bend. The water rushed down grayed stones in surging sprays.

"It's like the sky on a rainy day, sort of a cloudy white and misty gray," he remarked aloud.

"Whatever requires such weighty words?" Bea asked.

"I'm just thinking about the stream."

"Go right on thinking; I like your thinking."

They walked on attentive to the chirping of the birds and the crunching of leaves by the creatures in the underbrush.

"Enough thinking for now," Jal said. "I like to talk and look at the scenery; it's new every morning."

"That's how Bea and I feel each time we cruise this way, to pirate your phrase," Sammie said.

"For an opener, I'll tell you Callie's story, and Missy will get a mention," Bea said.

"Okay, we might let her tell us. Huh, Sammie, what do you think?" He lifted his brows in a puckish frown.

"You keep this joking up, and I'll sort out an ornery urchin." She rapped Jal on the head.

"Ow–ow, see what you've done to my head. Sammie, look at what she did?" Laughing, he said, "I can't help it; I do like to tease you."

Bea tapped him with a delicate kiss. "You're an incorrigible boy."

"Let me think for a while. In fact, I doubt if I'll ever get through thinking. Mom was evermore saying, 'Now think about what you do, Jal, before you do it.'"

Sammie, silent to this point, signaled to Bea. They smiled at one another and left Jal to his ruminations.

"I'm through thinking," Jal said when an hour had gone by. "I'd like to hear Callie's story now."

"You're on track to becoming a perfect little tyrant," Bea said in a voice of reproof. "Now you're ready. What happened to the genteel boy we started out with?"

"It's me, Bea," Jal said in an anxious tone. "I'm still me; I'm not a tyrant, its initiative. Dad said, 'You've got to have initiative in this world, Jal.'

"When I was younger I cried and stamped my feet if Mom said, 'No, Jal,' to something I wanted to do. 'You will not grow up to be a tyrant, Jal Valhyn. Tyrants come to a no good end.' I don't want to be a tyrant, Bea. I just want initiative."

"In that case, I beg your pardon and I'll begin." She gave him feather-like tap on the head. "For a contrite imp."

"Apparently, Callie was an abandoned baby, but we don't know for sure," she said. "Eli stumbled on her while he was completing an assignment in a seaside resort. She was a homeless youngster begging on the waterfront without relatives or friends. He gave her a donation and spoke kindly to her. By the end of a fortnight, she went along home with him. He consigned her to Molly's care on their arrival. 'My trust was absolute,' she says, when referring to her rescue.

"She lacked social skills, having spent most of her life alone. Mollie entrusted her to Porter's family. They're a lively bunch, and everyone is into community activities. She rapidly learned to be sociable and fitted right into the family. She asked Seraphina to teach her culinary skills. Molly filled in with lessons also. Within six months, she was serving up first-rate dishes. In a year or so, she became Molly's cooking assistant. She likes the outdoors despite her experience and goes on country rambles when her duties permit. She and Luellen often hike together.

"Callie has few memories of her early life. She told us that vague images flit into her mind when she's caring for a resident's baby. She survived by her wits and managed by 'tooth and claw.' That's how she describes her ordeal. 'My family now is a thousand fold, and I am forever grateful to be so happy,' she says of her present life.

"And Missy? Her given name is Louisa Victoria, as I said. About her story, you know as much as I do. I imagine she's a refugee from the war. I expect that the next the time we're together, she'll sing for us. That's my all-inclusive Callie and Missy findings. Wrapped up, as you said."

Jal laughed. "I must say, those were condensed stories. You need to slow down and take longer in telling them. Missy is pretty, isn't she? I hope she'll learn to speak up. Thank you, Bea. Mom taught me to say thank you when I was very young."

"Very young? Why, you aren't very old now."

"It seems to me I'm growing older by the day, especially listening to these stories you and Sammie tell me. Troubles, troubles, that's all I hear. I'm keen on those warriors, Mel and Cal. A warrior's life might suit me when I get older.

"Do you think I might be one, Sammie? They straighten out mixed-up messes; I'd like to chip in and help.

"I keep thinking of your story, about meeting Neda again. You want to be courageous and strong for her. I hope to be as strong as you are. And when Mom and Dad get to Grandfather Moutyn's, I'll impress them no end."

"You have impressed us, Jal, as a veritable little trouper on this journey. Without doubt, your mom and dad will think so too. Press on, old man," Sammie replied. "As to becoming a warrior, keep the wish in your heart. Wait and see."

"Press on? What does it mean?"

"Keep on doing what you're doing."

"About this country, Sammie—it seems most everyone I meet has had a lot of troubles."

"Overall, that's true," Sammie replied. "On this path in particular. But then, scores of willing settlers live here, as we mentioned previously. They read various materials or learn from diverse sources of emigration possibilities. Even though the WC restricted teaching on the subject, we gather up many from the byways. Those who enter are free to go or stay. "

"I can go back if I want to, Sammie?"

"Yes you may, Jal. Of course your parents would be notified and their wishes respected in any decision."

"I'm going to stay right here. I don't like it anymore in the country we left. "

"An astute choice for the discerning fellow you are, Jal. A settler you will be! I'll clue you in to a principal feature of your new home. The Owner King delegated to His personnel responsibilities for the world's inhabitants. Both Grandfather Moutyn and Syntee are on His staff. We are, and so are you, Jal. We, including you, share in the expansion of His empire.

"The long-term plan is to merge with Syntee's home country and bring the world you left behind into the alliance. This country's immigrants take part in furthering the goal of unification. Our job is to lead them in, the more the merrier. You embarked on the grand excursion of learning six days ago! A novice and yet promoting our vision."

"I'm in a mix-up again," Jal said. "I feel like my thoughts are a jumble. You did say I'd learn, Sammie, and my mind overflows since I met Syntee and you two. I know the things you tell me are true because of what's happened to me.

"You're speaking of bringing residents into this country. Some are born here, aren't they? For instance, Ora. She never had worries or problems. Do you think she might possibly understand a fellow who's gone through a lot of troubles, Sammie?"

Bea's eyes lit up with glee, and she rapped Sammie on the head. He said in a staid voice, "I am convinced that she would, Jal."

"I think so. How could a girl resist an enchanting fellow like you?" Bea said.

Sammie chided Bea for rapping his head. "You quit that, Bea. Can't a lad be serious?"

He picked up the discussion where he had left off. "About our bringing into this country...Jal. Four Guardians, appointed by the Owner, are in charge of the ones who enter. We've mentioned Ethan. Syntee, you've met, and how! The two others are Anthiela, the Guardian of the West, and Lemiel, the Guardian of the East. In fact, Bea and I are appointees under Syntee's guidance. We met Anthiela and Lemiel on one occasion, but not their messengers. We assisted Mel and Cal when Syntee gave us a directive. Don't even try to sort all this out. Grandfather Moutyn is just the right teacher for a young man of initiative."

"Now you're teasing me, Sammie," Jal said to him suspiciously.

"On the contrary," Sammie said, rumpling his hair.

"Sammie, I've been thinking about Uhlin and Cousin Tabor. Do you think Syntee might invite them to live here? Eli might go and talk to them."

"Not a farfetched idea. It's very possible, Jal. However, your mom and dad are apt to clue them in. Your wish may be granted within the year. Add it to your waits and sees."

"Time for lunch," Bea said during a lull in the conversation. "This seems to be a good spot to sit without wrinkling my clothes. Aren't you hungry?"

Jal put his fingers to his lips and motioned to Sammie, "We can go farther, for an hour or two, if you wish, Bea."

She regarded him with compressed lips and distrustful eyes, "Why, you're a little prankster. Nuts to you and Sammie. Let's sit over there."

She took off for a grassy clearing by the stream. "Here, you guys. Relaxation time. Trifling chitchat only."

"You're sort of bossy, Bea, but I like you so much, I don't mind. Mom is bossy too. So, I'll quit talking and eat my lunch, my jam tart also, if you don't mind."

"A lot of minds and sos in you today. In fact, I don't object. So sit and eat."

21

When they were on the path again, Sammie said, "Let's talk about the Grand Chasm we have to cross today."

"What's the Grand Chasm?" Jal asked. "Another creepy thing?" His earlier thought of Sammie's reference to a "desolate countryside" came to mind. "You mean the desolate countryside, Sammie?"

"Yes, throw that in too, but let me explain the Grand Chasm."

"Bea could you help me in this?"

She shook her head from side to side and said, "All yours, Sammie."

He took a deep breath. "Here goes. The chasm is not so grand; it's more like a ravine with a bridge over its width. The bridge is quite long, with no lower or upper rung supports, and moves with your steps. Nothing to fear; we've crossed at divers seasons and times and never a pilgrim lost," he said in a reassuring tone.

Jal slowed his pace to think over the things Sammie had said. *A Grand Chasm. What a lot I've learned in just a few days, though it seems much longer, years and years.* His thoughts went back to the hours he had wandered the village alone. *Grand Chasms are one jolt and a quaver compared to those days. A baby dragon, a whack off the bridge.*

He gave his attention to the landscape and the changing scenery. The trees were dense and wild on the other side of the stream, with huge ferns growing under them. Tangled brush and shrubs covered the open ground. But on the path, the sunlight fell through the tree leaves, and the water gurgled and flowed, reliable constants.

"Sammie, does it rain in this country? It's been sunny since we started out," Jal asked.

"Naturally, the rains come like everywhere else. This area, dried out and cheerless, detours around our realm, and water is in short supply. The stone bridge spanning a skimpy creek is not far off. Soon after, we'll be at the Grand Chasm."

Seeing Jal's bewildered expression, he said, "Wait."

"What a strange place, Sammie. Does anyone live here?"

"No, not even one. This region is the hinterland, the desolate countryside I mentioned. Perhaps someday pioneers may flock to the area. Who can tell?"

A bridge made of one serrated stone block loomed in front of them. To Jal, the bridge transported them into an inexplicable alien land. They stepped off into a minute meadow ringed by a stand of trees in twisted, bent shapes. Wild blackberry bushes in untidy and compacted growth covered the ground. The path, clearly marked, ran beside the stream and sang its usual cheery notes.

What appeared to be a short distance through the petite meadow was far from short to Jal. To him, hours and yet more hours were going by. "What's with this meadow?" he said plaintively. Uneasy, he moved closer to Sammie, who gave him a comforting pat. *I'm glad Sammie and Bea are here,* he thought with relief.

He knew hours weren't passing or else the sun would be farther down the horizon. A hilly terrain appeared in the distance, and a bridge that ran the length of a seemingly undersized ravine. Baffled by his experience with the meadow, he kept his thoughts to himself. *Wait a while; I'll ask later. There I go with the wait thing!*

"Is that the Grand Chasm, Sammie, with the piddling bridge?"

"Wait, you'll see,"

Seems I have waited hours, Jal thought as they approached the Grand Chasm.

Four vine cables, two on each side, stretched the width of the chasm. Four iron posts fitted into granite secured the cables on each side of the ravine. The bridge rungs woven of vines linked into the lower cables in a crisscross pattern. *Indeed, a long bridge, no use to quibble,* Jal thought with chagrin.

"Don't be frightened, Jal," Bea said, speeding to him. "The bridge is strong and vastly underrated as piddling." She patted his head.

Jal hesitated, gripped Sammie's hand, and put one foot on the bridge and then the other. He felt a shifting movement beneath his feet and clung to Sammie's hand with his eyes tightly closed.

The bridge swayed back and forth with each step they took. Hours appeared to be going by yet again. *Will we ever get over? I can't decide which is longest, this bridge or the meadow.* He opened his eyes when Bea said, "We made it, Jal."

Jal let go of his tension with a sigh and released Sammie's hand. "Thank goodness we're through with that! I've had enough for one day," he declared, exhaling noisily.

"It's quite arduous, I agree," Sammie replied. "Atta boy, enough for me too."

"I clutch Sammie's head in such a squeeze, it's a miracle he can see to move his feet," Bea said meekly. "I seal my eyes tight like you, Jal, until we get over the bridge."

"I'm glad to know I'm not the only one scared stiff, to quote my Uncle Joulh."

"That bridge and meadow! Wait till I tell Mom and Dad, Sammie. 'You're round the bend, Jal,' Dad will say to me."

The path appeared with the rhythmic burblings of the stream. The overhanging branches of the trees screened the path and the sunlight trickled through the leaves. A sense of ordinary reality restored Jal's good humor.

"What a strange experience. Can you tell me why, Sammie? I thought we'd never get through the meadow, and then came the bridge! Hours, infinite hours! The sun hardly budged on the horizon. So, it can't have been so very long."

"You're right," Sammie replied. "We don't know the why, Jal. Crossing the meadow and the bridge doesn't bother Bea or me. Grandfather Moutyn can answer your questions better than we can."

"My baffle bag is chockfull," Jal said. "Boy! Grandfather Moutyn has a lot of questions to answer."

Bea interrupted. "Let's sit awhile with our friend stream. I'm tired."

"You're tired, Bea? Why, you sat on Sammie's head the entire day. We're the ones worn out. If Sammie is as weary as I am...are you done in, Sammie? I'm washed out from being so scared while we crossed the bridge. Does your hand hurt, Sammie?"

"Washed out, are you? Anyway, let's rest. You two could use a break. And for your information, you naughty young'un, I do get wacked from sitting on Sammie's head," Bea said and then perched on a rock that jutted out from the stream.

Sammie cut in, "If you two quit jabbering long enough, I'll tell you I'm tired but in perfectly good form. To answer your question, Jal, I'm relieved you weathered the crossing with your humor intact. A good night's sleep is in order to salvage the numb hand you clutched and the head Bea tried to crunch."

He took a seat and ate a fruit. "I like a fruit once in a while and a cookie."

"I like water every day," Bea said, restating Sammie's words. "You and Jal can eat the fruit and the cookies."

"I endorse Sammie's likings. Mom said, when I disagreed with Dad, 'I endorse your father's idea, Jal.' That meant I'd better obey."

"Your mama is sensible; it's best to obey one's parents," Sammie said.

He stood up and brushed crumbs off his shirt. "Let's be going. We'll soon be at the guesthouse. Tomorrow afternoon we'll reach your new home. We can ease up on the trail—even have a morning's sleep-in if you wish."

22

They walked on in tune with the sounds of the woods and the cadence of the stream. To Jal, the beats of the water were distinct and different. He heard the diverse notes rising and falling in a musical composition. The sun moved toward the horizon, casting pink tints on the water. "Pink lemonade," he said. "I had pink lemonade the time Mom and I went to visit Milya. She lived hundreds of miles from us, and Mom booked passage on the C Tube.

"Why not take the C Tube, Sammie? We'd be at Grandfather Moutyn's in a few minutes."

"You tell him, Sammie, about our old-fashioned ways," Bea said.

"The rule is foot travel in this country, but Syntee ascertains the need," Sammie replied. "In reference to your former country—for generations walking has been the preferred means for local travel. The WC authorized it to instill an awareness of the natural world. Individual transport, or cars, became passé. The political authorities and architectural designers relocated services within a reasonable walking distance. Thus, suburbia morphed into villages."

"I do walk most places, Sammie, or ride my bike. On overlong trips we took the fastest way, and this is a pretty long trip."

"If we had taken the C Tube, what then? You're a reflective fellow; think on the subject and tell us your thoughts."

"Right off, and most important, I wouldn't have gotten to know you and Bea. Your friendship is worth a dozen C Tubes. Sammie, I'm grateful for walking and all the friends I've met. Syntee is amazing, isn't He?"

"Good, Jal, you are a quick learner. Talking about the C Tube...You may not have learned its beginnings yet."

"No, next year's civics, Sammie."

"Okay, a shift to developing rapid transit speeded up when the WC authorized walking. The C Tube evolved—that is, movement by air pressure. For countrywide and international travel, it has no equal. Much faster than the old planes that flew by air. The M (magnetic) trains are for local and long distance ground transport. Ocean voyages are hydrogen fuelled. I like walking best. Nature profits, and so do its two-legged inhabitants. Anyway, our assignments are by pathways."

"In this country, no one arrives by the C-Tube," Bea added. "Our duties stress feet on the ground, or the wings. Only me by wings. Sammie decided on walking when we entered Syntee's service."

"Guess I'm to wait for you to explain that?" Jal said.

"Yes, for now. Look!"

A cottage of buff-colored stone with a plain front and two windows offered an agreeable prospect to the tired travelers. The cabin was larger than the previous ones with two bedrooms, and there was a bath in each. Bea's miniature bedroom, the outside carved in the shape of a butterfly, included a tiny basin and a shower.

"Mine," Bea said. "Grandfather Moutyn sketched the plans, and one of his artisans built it especially for me. I like sharing the stream with you two, but a girl needs privacy in her bath."

The table was set for three, and food was on a warming tray. "This time we missed the delivery by minutes," Sammie said.

Jal touched the clothes on his and Sammie's beds. "I think whoever brought the things wants to keep us guessing. Mom did the same thing on my birthday. 'I keep you guessing, Jal. If I didn't you wouldn't like your presents half so much,' she said. The food and clothes are presents, so I skim the subject and do my guesswork."

Bea chuckled. "Mystery, mystery, the lambkin is gripped by mysteries." She brushed his face with her wings. "In good time, you'll learn. Syntee devised the guesthouses and specified their location. Those who live in the area accept responsibility for their maintenance. Even Ora might be a helper."

Sammie said, "The shelter and the food are not such a mystery, or a miracle. Those who live nearest to our stopover for the night stock our cupboard, as we said earlier. Others contribute to the clothes and personal items included in the service."

"It's still a miracle to me, Sammie. I hardly had enough to eat last week, like Bea in her summer drought. Mine dried up too; the stores had nothing to sell. Each evening, we find these things and I begin to think, *Someone cares for us.*

"Dad says, 'Thank your mom, Jal. She makes our home happy with loving care and good cooking.' I forgot lots of times, but I never did on her birthday. I'd like to say thank you to whoever it is."

"We've left notes of thanks, Jal; they will have to suffice in lieu of the personal," Bea said.

Sammie added, "We do know Grandfather Moutyn is responsible for this guesthouse, and the goodies are delivered by a villager."

"Do you think, Sammie, Grandfather Moutyn will let me be a helper? The task might be fun."

"Keep the thought, Jal; perhaps you can. Better, wait until you schedule your studies with Mom and Dad's input. Once that is set, other pursuits are available for trial and error. You might try out the role of a helper."

Jal put aside his questions and asked about dinner. Bea gave him a swift glance and sat down at the table. "I'm hungry too. I've been waiting for you to say something."

"Sammie and I know you're hungry."

Bea fluttered her wings at him and said between gulping sounds, "Back in a sec." She entered her bedroom and closed the door.

"Let's do a wash up and pacify the call of the food with Bea," Sammie said.

Bea reappeared after a brief interval. "There, a pepper up. A shower after a day of walking. Let's eat guys."

Jal, distracted by his brown bread, pasta, and salad, failed to see Bea tap dancing on Sammie's head.

"I see you like to eat," Bea tittered.

Jal smiled. "I learned from you. The food is so scrummy. Notice I didn't say anything about your 'walking' quip today."

"I'll ignore that statement for the moment. Umm—Ooo... this nectar tastes different; I know it's an unbroken repeat three times a day," she said, slurping from her cup.

"My grains are the same; I'm not familiar with the selection and mixing methods. I'll have to ask Porter at our next gathering. Cecil and Ben do the flavors, and that's the extent of my knowledge," Sammie said.

"Maybe you'll see them before we do, Jal, and you can tell us."

"I will, Sammie. My vittles are lip-smacking scrumptious, like the jam tart at lunch." Jal took a drink of milk and glanced at Bea and then smacked his lips.

"You are an ornery young'un. Spying on me, aren't you?"

"Don't ask me. I'm learning when to keep my mouth shut, like Sammie does." He smiled at her.

She eyed him doubtfully and tapped him briskly on the tip of his nose.

"Don't push your luck, you and Sammie; misfortune will befall, and it won't be to me."

Once the dishes and the table were neatened, they sat on the steps of the cabin for a short while. The dusk deepened, and the stars filled the night sky.

Jal, ruminating on their coming separation, said in a mournful tone, "I'll miss you both most dreadfully."

Bea gave his hair a tug, and Sammie smoothed it down. "Cheer up, Jal; we'll pop round so often you'll give us a get lost sign," Bea said. "That is, once you're into your studies and meeting interesting friends."

"That can never be, I will miss you. I feel better because you keep saying we'll visit each other often. I 'm not as sad about Mom, Dad, and Uncle Joulh. I do expect them to roll up any day. At any rate I don't cry."

"Yes, you're growing by leaps and bounds, with a head full of learning to be sorted out in good time. And roll ups for Sammie and me too, eh, Sammie? "

"Pronto. Now for a roll in the stream to relax our travel-weary bodies. And off to bed we go," Sammie replied.

"Goody." Bea soared ahead of them. "I love night dips in the stream. A delightful extravagance we seldom indulge in on our missions. This makes twice on this trip. Here's a prime place."

"She scouts out the places for dips on our trips," Sammie said.

"She learned her skills on those scouting sprees for food, eh?" Jal said.

"You're an impudent young'un." With a titter, Bea gave his hair a tug, flew straight up, and back down into the pool.

Laughing, Sammie and Jal entered the shallow pool and started a splashing contest.

"You two young'uns," Bea shrilled. "You guys are drenching me. My hair is all mussed. Look at what you did to me. I'm wringing wet." She rapped both on the head. They laughed and threw more water at her.

Afterward they sat reflecting on the multitude of stars. "An excess of treats in the sky tonight, Jal." Sammie pointed to a cluster of stars and sketched the outline of the big dipper with his finger.

Jal kept his eyes on the outline and said, "For the first time ever, I recognize the shape. Uncle Joulh and I went to a planetarium. But the night sky here? I know how Cecil felt when he viewed the stars. There's no comparison. This is fabulous!"

A shooting star streaked across the heavens and burst into a great shower of light. "A performance just for us," Bea remarked. Clusters of fiery gems sprayed the sky as they gazed in silent wonder.

Sammie broke the enchanted spell by saying, "Time for bed."

They made their way back to the cabin. Bea said good night and went to her room. Sammie prepared lunches for the next day and then toppled into bed. Jal speedily descended into a deep slumber that brought dreams of the Big Dipper and the stars into his restful night's sleep.

Seventh Day
23

Jal awoke in the early morning and remembered he was to make breakfast for Bea. He tiptoed to the cabinet, rummaged for the food in the half-light, and stubbed his toe against the table. "Ow," he said and woke Sammie up. He put the food down and hobbled over to the bed with his finger to his lips, "Shh...shh. Breakfast for Bea. I don't want to wake her."

He poured the nectar into a violet-colored cup and set a bowl of grains in place. "For you, Sammie; this one is mine." He filled another bowl with cereal. The table laid, he knocked on Bea's door.

"Ready for breakfast, sleepy head?"

He heard a peevish grumbling. "What's got into you, Jal Valhyn, getting up in the middle of the night?"

"The middle of the night, Bea? It's time to get up for breakfast," he replied in a hurt tone.

She peeked out and looked at his table preparations. "Why, Jal, you darling you, I do repent! Forgive me for being grumpy." She came out, kissed him on the head, and went back into her room. Reappearing in a violet-colored silk robe, she picked up her cup. "My best robe, just for you, sets off the cup.

"And…for you, Bea." He gave her a lilac napkin dotted with violets.

"You are a pet, you sweet one. You found my stash, to match my robe." Bea sipped her nectar with umm-umms and daintily wiped her lips.

Jal, contented with her response, concentrated on his own breakfast.

Sammie fastened the cabin door on their exit with the remark, "The comforts of a mini home. Last night on the trail, Jal."

"The best, Sammie, the cabin and the trail. I'll try not to be too gloomy. Distract me with a tale."

The haziness of the morning receded as they reached the pathway. The woodland creatures and the birds seemed to be chattering more than ever. *Gabbing and sharing their day's work,* Jal said to himself. *They must have their troubles too.* The thought reminded him of his parents and his uncle. *Eli will bring them to me, so I'll wait. Syntee has told them where I am.* He breathed out a wisp of air and felt a rapping on his head.

"Hello, down there. Want to join us? I've been at this for some time. You seem well able to distract yourself. No help needed."

"Sorry, Bea, I was thinking again."

"Our leisurely walk to appreciate the critters, then on to Monty's story."

A picture of the odd, yet likeable, being in Eli's home flitted into Jal's mind. "Yes, I would like to know Monty's story and how he came to live with Eli. But 'our walk' is a bit much since you sit on Sammie's head most of the time."

"I had to get your attention," she countered, reseating herself. "Walking is for the tall with long legs. I have short legs, but they're very shapely." She gestured by tossing her hair, stood on tiptoe, and spun around.

Sammie and Jal glanced at each other with a slight smile.

"Indeed, your legs are shapely, and Sammie's head is the showoff place," Jal said.

"That's my boy," Sammie said. "You're more on your toes by the day."

Melodious notes fell in a varied repetition from the stream, as if to impart its joy to them. Siftings of light on the path sparkled and flashed before them in an energetic ballet dance. "A recital just for us," Jal commented.

"No call to get your attention for Act 1." Bea gave him a pat on the head. "No thump necessary."

"I'm ready for Monty's story," Jal said after an hour or so.

"Okay, I'll tackle this one, Sammie."

"Where to begin? At his opening act, I suppose. Montague was born in a Western country on a large estate. For eons, his grandfather and then his father had been the overseer. Monty was in line to succeed to the position, but the world war stuck its oar in.

"Monty delighted in the estate's way of life. The comings and goings of the Great People thrilled him to no end. Even more, he exulted in his headwaiter status during the annual holiday balls. The gentry for miles around attended in their top hats and tails. 'The suits are so dashing, Dad. I wish I had one,' he often said.

"His greatest sense of satisfaction, though, came from his monthly circuits of the estate grounds—a duty he had performed since the age of fifteen. In this way, he proceeded through leisurely and contented days. He was in his late teens when reports of a war began to filter in. Taken up with the tasks of daily life, newscasts of problems elsewhere seemed a million miles away. 'Do your duty, young fellow, and pay no mind to the gossip of the outside world,' his dad advised him.

"Hostilities flared up on his country's borders, and with the WC's failure in arbitration, the conflict moved inland. Caught up in his farm work, and the monthly patrols, Monty paid scant attention to the rumors of the war.

"One evening he came in from a day's patrol to a dreadful uproar. Armed men were everywhere, and in a panic, he headed for his home. A soldier grabbed him and shoved him into a lineup.

"In the early-morning hours, the enemy had attacked and captured the village. The residents were ordered to assemble in the commons square and were then marched to the estate grounds. The proprietor and his family, as well as Monty's parents, entered an armored vehicle on command. The neighbor, who informed him of the day's happenings, said a soldier had mentioned a prison camp as the van moved off."

"That must have been dreadful for Monty," Jal said. "At least we escaped before the war got to our home."

"True, Jal, so true," Bea replied.

"However, to resume…Monty, panic stricken and numb with pain, was pushed into the back of a military truck. They traveled through the night and arrived at a prison camp in mid-morning. In the camp, he set off in search of his parents, but they were not among the internees. New prisoners entered daily, and for months, he questioned each arrival. Eventually he learned of their detention in a fortress constructed for prominent officials and leaders in government.

"His captors considered him harmless and somewhat daft when he began a morning march around the walled encampment. The soldiers on daily patrol ignored him after a few weeks. Monty cautiously scoured the area for an outlet. He noticed a weakness in the iron fence that bounded the prison camp. A loose railing was a possible escape route if it could be forced apart. He determined to try and waited for an opportunity."

"You finish the tale, Sammie?" Bea said.

"Fine, Bea. Off we go," Sammie replied.

"On a day when only one guard patrolled the boundaries of the camp, Monty followed him. He slowed his steps and kept out of sight until the guard had gotten past the defective railing. Without further ado, he bent the rail aside and plunged through the fence. He sprinted toward the heavily forested woodlands that skirted the camp. He continued to run wildly to no purpose or plan into the middle of the forest. He floundered about in dark thickets and brushwood during the night and the following day.

"He became ill and feverish after two days without sleep, food, or water. Eli found him unable to speak coherently, summoned medical help, and sent him to Porter's family. Monty regained full consciousness a week later. He recognized Eli, but his past is a closed book that has never been reopened to him. Eli gradually told him the story of their meeting and suggested that he stay and make his home on the farm.

"Monty recovered his physical strength, though the past remains elusive. Even so, when puzzled by a tug of memory, a voice, or a scent, he sits alone deep in thought. But these moments pass. After he was well, he asked Eli for permission to patrol the boundaries of the property. Eli gave him an old blunderbuss, a replica and harmless. He also asked for a top hat and tails. The abiding tug of memory.

"His rounds often find him at dark on the outer edges of the farm. A resident will put him up for the night after ringing Molly. Eli continues to search for his parents, but to date they are still missing. The evidence points to their decease, no doubt in prison.

"We're familiar with his story because Eli pieced it together from diverse informants to give Monty closure. He's content in Eli's home and is a valued member of the community."

"How sad," Jal said. "I'm glad Monty is safe and cheerful now. I'm not the only one with sadness, am I?"

"No, Jal, you aren't," Sammie said. "The house of trouble is crowded with many inhabitants, but the house grows brighter and a little more spacious when we help each other bear the troubles."

"Sammie, the things you say need a lot of thought before I can talk with you on the subjects. I expect that sometime I'll be ready—ready to talk about the Owner too. Wait and see, like you tell me!"

"I'll wait and see, Jal. I'm sure Bea and I won't be disappointed."

His mind filled with thoughts and questions, Jal fell to the rear. Sammie stopped until he caught up.

"A few days ago you asked me how Eli gets the info when someone is in trouble. Did you forget our chat? "

"Hah! Forget? So tell me the classified hush-hush you keep under wraps."

"Go back to the day you asked me how I knew Mel and Cal were at the guesthouse. Peek at my forehead. See anything?"

"No, not even a widget," Jal replied.

"Put your finger here," Sammie insisted. "Feel the wee dot above my right eye."

"There's a white speck on your head. Imagine! Something smaller than Bea's lavatory!"

"Go, check Bea's forehead, and ignore the sour expression she's giving you."

"A white dot; I'm surprised it isn't pink. Don't rap me, you pint-sized tweeter. You're spiky! Sorry, Bea, it's fun to tease you."

"Pint-sized, am I, and spiky? I admit I'm a mite on the itty bitty side, but you—"

"Break," Sammie said. "The speck is an intouch tool that the Owner devised. Mel sent me a memo on the evening before he and Cal met with us. A messenger calls Eli when emergencies crop up, and Monty was certainly a major crisis. Hold on, and you'll learn how the tool functions in this country. Bea mentioned once about the Tots we have. A gamut of others is on order for your learning."

"I'm glad you told me. I can mark off one entry in my *wander bag*. I stress *wander* because Mom said, 'You wander from room to room when you're thinking, Jal.' My head really gets in a whirl! You two keep saying, 'Wait and see.' So, now my mind is stuffed full of wandering things, and if that wasn't enough, you stowed in the Owner."

Bea smiled and gently rapped him on the head. "Don't fuss at the stowage, Jal. In good time, clarity will erase your fuzzy wanderings. The steps from A to Z go up to lofty heights. Just think—you've already learned so many things. Line upon line, here a little, there a little, to quote our Book of Authority."

Jal thought, *True, I stash away dabs of learning, and one or two I grasp every day. Maybe I'm quarter of the way through the A's.* He sighed and transferred his attention to the scenery. The leaves moved faintly in the light wind. The stream's burbling grew softer and richer in tone.

24

The path looped round a bend, and a pocket-sized glade appeared. Wild flowers grew in profusion, and a rock bench beckoned from the bank of the stream.

"Lunch at last," Bea said gleefully. "My hunger pangs need pacifying. This is our special spot; we'll eat here."

"How lovely," Jal said. "Mom said those words when she got a new dress. The one she wore on my birthday is the color of those white stones. At the bottom, look." He directed their attention to the stones under the water.

Sammie, setting out the lunch, nodded. "A lovely color for a dark-haired mother. She might wear it for our benefit. Bea and I intend to meet her soon."

"Let's sit and take our fill of all things lovely," Bea said whimsically.

Jal paid scant attention to her words. He sat brooding on their coming separation. *In the morning, they leave.* Tears came to his eyes; he got up from the bench and moved closer to the stream.

"Why, Jal, whatever's the matter now?" Bea inquired in a solicitous tone.

"You and Sammie will be going home tomorrow, won't you?"

"Yes, on plan. We can't be with you daily, but our drop ins may be more than enough for you. We'll be at the gathering in less than a month. Uncle Joulh may be on his way in the interim, and you'll be too excited to give us a thought. Another thing… Sammie and I are part of your family. We aren't going anywhere."

"Then, if you aren't going anywhere, I might as well give you the leftovers in my cache of thoughts," Jal replied in a petulant tone. "That waits jabber…wait…wait. It's all you two yammer every day."

"What can we say?" Sammie said. "To integrate learning takes time. We also wait for many things while pressing on with our missions. Yes, there are troubles in our life but lasting joys too. Now there, my last lecture of the day," Sammie said with a wry grin, touching Jal's face in a tender gesture.

Jal muttered under his breath, "Sorry, Sammie." In a softened tone of voice, he said, "I get so mixed up. I'm mad at everything sometimes."

"Your feelings are valid, Jal; you've endured a lot in a short time. Messed up aplenty, home disrupted, mom and dad gone, and to add the frosting, an uncle missing. Bea and I, not unlike your parents, are obligated to duties we must honor. No wonder you're angry.

"Coping with a mix of painful feelings is a study in itself, and a tidy up is an active effort over an obstacle course. We'd be poor indeed without feelings. If we didn't have any we might be like...but we really don't know what we'd be like, do we? Feelings, the pleasant and the painful, seem to come in one bag. They're a package deal, alas."

"Mom sent me to my room when I got mad, Sammie. 'I recommend that you calm yourself, dear, and think about why you're angry,' she said. I figured out it happened when she refused me something I wanted. Now it's the same thing. I want you and Bea to stay with me, and Mom and Dad to be here. I even want the war to be gone."

"A worthy analysis, Jal."

"Sammie, I don't always think about my anger. I pitched a doozy of a fit when Dad told me that he and Mom had to go into the military. "

"In such a case, a doozy may be called for, Jal. Your mom has begun a good work in teaching you self-control. We must strive to channel our emotions in ways that will be constructive for our growth. Anger, in particular, can lead to ruin. If let to grow, it can explode like the atom bomb in olden times. Just consider the worldwide war!

"Recall, we spoke of building blocks a while ago in the recycling of our emotions. Anger is an element in making our blocks; its stimulating force, if rightly used, will contribute to a well-built structure. I'm talking of things important to our growth, Jal."

"Let me point out," Bea interjected, "this is the first time you've spoken to us of being angry. Why not in the past days?"

Taken aback, Jal deliberated on Bea's statement. "You're right, Bea. I think I was afraid to—at the start anyhow. I thought you and Sammie wouldn't like me. I'm not so miserable since we met, but I do want you to stay with me. I am vexed because you two are going home. A fellow has to tell you, doesn't he? And for your info, most of the time I feel downright cheerful."

"My dear boy," Sammie said, "a model champ you'll be in this brand-new country. Within a week, a growing list of lifelong friends can be posted to your bedroom wall. Bea said it; we aren't going anywhere."

"Since we're on the subject of Grandfather Moutyn, would you like dabs of his story?" Bea inquired.

"Wait a minute," he replied, "until I finish this sandwich and think on what you said." He watched the ripples of light skimming the top of the water and thought, *I'll store their words in my memory cache. I want to be like Sammie.*

Bea and Sammie searched his face on the way back to the path. Jal smiled at them. "Now about Grandfather Moutyn, please. Thinking can wait a while"

"Go ahead, you tell him, Bea."

"Seems there are lots of things for us to learn yet," she began. "We've never plumbed the mystery of his arrival in the village. Ages perhaps, though jots and tittles are what we know. We intend to ask him when we're with him, but the time scarpers off and we're heading home. He is fond of simple structures and designed the buildings on the premises. Syntee and he collaborate periodically on joint projects.

"Grandfather Moutyn oversees assorted facilities for most scientific and academic education. On site are also skilled crafts and artisan complexes along with centers for agriculture, vine-yards, and horticulture. Students from various nations come to train and devote their skills to this country's expansion. Your innate likings indicate the direction of your future. The diversi-fied areas of learning in this country provide an entree to your prospective career. Sammie and I mean to verify every single interest of yours."

"I recognize one now," Jal replied. "What I want is for you and Sammie to visit me often. Promise? I guess one of those widgets you wear is wanted."

Sammie waggled his head in response. "You're targeted for unexpected stopovers. You have our word. As for the widget, Mom and Dad are inputters. Wait!"

He motioned to Bea, who said, "No doubt about it, Jal. Taken up with your studies, new friends and lots of activities, time will fly. You'll look up and there we'll be popping up on a pop-in." She batted her wings at Jal, and giggled.

"Frequent visits are well and good but every day ones would be better. Okay—okay," he said, in response to her sad expression. "To please you, I'll table the nagging for now."

The path began to wind through open fields. The tall grasses by the stream swayed back and forth in the afternoon sun. "I wonder where Eli is," Jal said.

"He's been nabbed for a taxing task, no doubt; maybe he'll stop by this evening," Sammie replied in a bantering tone.

"I wouldn't mind. In fact, I would like to see him. I was kinda scared at first. He's big and fierce looking, but once I saw his face I wasn't afraid. You told me, Sammie, that Eli gave up his kingdom for this country. Kings have humongous riches and honors, don't they? Why didn't he want to be a king?"

"Because he fell in love, Jal. He found a love greater than his kingdom, a love for the King, Most High. Think on the words of your mother, 'The cord of love is strong.' The King, our Owner, holds the cord of a thousand strands interweaving our lives. You're at the beginning of a grand expedition, a cavalcade of learning."

"Thank you, Sammie. Now I know where Mom heard about the cord of love."

"A mother's love is reflective of our Owner's love, Jal."

25

The path leveled out after ascending a short rise and then broadened into a graveled road leading downward. Sammie motioned to a picturesque vista that appeared to be mounted in a timeless frame. "Our journey's end. Behold! Your new home, Jal."

Jal surveyed the wide-ranging scene, captivated by its beauty. Feelings of his past losses and hope for the future battled for dominance within him for a long minute. Hope won and seemed to be contained in the peaceful scene he gazed upon. About twenty stone cottages formed a quadrangle surrounding an open space of green. A large building with a glassed-in front sat in the center of the green space. To the right stood a roomy U-shaped house built of warm yellow stone. Beyond were sweeping fields with diverse vegetation. They descended the hill, crossed the stream by a wooden bridge, and entered a sylvan path that led into the village.

A workshop with "Cobbler" written on the door stood about two hundred yards from the yellow stone house. A man with platinum hair and undetermined age appeared in the doorway. Sammie walked faster.

"Whoa, Sammie, slow down. You're jiggling me."

"Sorry, Bea, hold on; we're here."

She grabbed Sammie's beak and said in her loudest tone, "Grandfather Moutyn, trail's end. Your parcel is intact."

He sauntered toward them and spoke in a voice both commanding and pleasing to the ear. "Hallo, Bea and Sammie, I've been on sentry duty since midday.

"Welcome, Jal, to your new home. The trail's end, as Bea says."

Jal remained stationary to appraise the person advancing towards them. He saw a slender man of medium height with silver white hair. Dark blue eyes with crinkly laughter lines were set in a tanned and amiable face. Jal examined him from head to toe and then smiled, pleased with Grandfather Moutyn's appearance.

"We'll have a refreshing drink before dinner, Jal," he said as they entered the U-shaped yellow stone house. "Let's go into the dining room. Aunt Letty is making citrus lemonade and a special meal for us this evening. We might leaf through a page of your journey while waiting."

Jal hung back to avoid speaking. He whispered to Sammie, "You tell him."

"No. Stage time for you, Jal," Sammie replied.

A matronly woman with a cheerful face framed by dark brown hair came into the room carrying a tray of mugs. "Not long to wait, GM. "

"Bea and Sammie, a visit has been months overdue. And a prized cargo you're bringing us today," she said.

Jal, grateful for the reprieve, advanced to meet her. She leaned down and kissed him on the forehead. "It is a joy to have you as a member of our family, Jal."

She gave a drink to Sammie and Jal and said to Bea, "A mug of your own, my dear." She extended a mini porcelain vessel to her and took a seat with a signal to Father Moutyn. "A stint of nattering can wait," she said. "The three of you scurry upstairs and do a tidy up for dinner. Jal might like to see his room."

"Of course, he might," Grandfather Moutyn said. "Off you go, Jal, for a shower and a change of clothes."

"Mattie will show you to your rooms," Aunt Letty said. "By the way, Eli is coming to dinner this evening."

"And Tyhe. Is he due?" Sammie asked.

"Tyhe is expected any minute and is staying overnight," she replied.

Grandfather Moutyn smiled with twinkling eyes while she chattered. "She runs our household, Jal. It's best to obey her."

"Where is Dottie, Aunt Letty?" Bea cut in.

"Off on an errand. She's rushing to finish her chores to free up time for your gabfest. We'll catch up on other news at dinner, but first…"

"Mattie, say hello to our friends." She went into the kitchen and came out with a short, chubby adolescent in tow.

"Mattie is newly enrolled as a family member. He's helpful and kindly and a pleasant friend for Jal." She shook her head benignly. "Please show them to their rooms, Mattie."

Mattie took them upstairs, opened the first door off the stair landing, and ushered them inside. "This will be your room, Jal." The walls were a pale blue, and a green wool rug lay on the wooden floor. A patchwork quilt of green and yellow bordered in blue covered the bed.

Curtains of yellow, green, and blue framed the window, which opened on a lovely outdoor scene. Jal crossed the room and viewed the stream running by the side of a small flower garden. *I'm glad you're just outside my window,* he thought, noting a desk and chair in one corner of the room and a bookcase with study materials to the right of it. To the left was a bathroom with a glass enclosed shower.

Mattie said with a smile, "Come here, Jal." An assortment of clothes was hanging in the closet. and two pairs of shoes were on a rack. "We knew you didn't have time to bring yours."

"Be happy in this home, Jal," Bea said. "And wear the green polo shirt for dinner."

"Advice to be followed, old fellow," Sammie said and pulled the shirt off the hangar.

They went out to the landing, and Mattie opened two doors adjacent to Jal's room. He motioned to Bea and Sammie and said, "These are yours." He opened a door on an extra-small bedroom decorated in shades of blue and yellow.

"My bed has a yellow coverlet, my favorite color. And pink in dresses," Bea said to Jal. "Our same rooms. Thank you, Mattie."

"And mine is green and white, if you're wondering," Sammie said, and went into his room.

Jal showered in his new bath with mixed feelings of gratefulness and sadness. *A million years ago, another bath*, he thought. *What a peculiar week!*

There was knock on his door, and Sammie came in. "Hurry up, old fellow, Bea is rarin' to eat. That green shirt sets your black curly hair off. Wait 'til Bea gets a gander at it." Jal finished dressing, and they went downstairs.

"That's much better," Aunt Letty said. "One more fruit drink? Grandfather Moutyn will be back in a jiffy. He's reviewing a project that needs his approval by the end of the day."

"'Pon my honor," Bea said. "Aunt Letty, will you look at the green shirt Jal has on? Sets his black curly hair right off, doesn't it?"

"Perfectly," Aunt Letty replied.

"Thanks," Jal said. "I suspect you heard Sammie say that, Bea."

She pretended she didn't hear by saying. "Here's Mattie."

He brought the drinks to them, and picking up the tray, went toward the kitchen. At Jal's inquisitive look, Aunt Letty said, "He's shy. He's much better—" She broke off as Grandfather Moutyn came in.

"Is your room satisfactory, Jal?" he asked. "Tell us if you need anything."

"No, I can't think of any need, but I do have a question. Could we go for a walk while we wait to eat?"

"My pleasure, Jal," Grandfather Moutyn replied.

"I must be excused," Aunt Letty said. "Dinner...maybe, Mattie..."

"Would you like to go for a walk, Mattie?" she asked from the dining room doorway.

"Okay. I'll put my walking shoes on."

Grandfather Moutyn escorted the procession into the village center. "Most of the folks will be at our gathering this week, Jal. A number of young people will be there. The news of your arrival has been percolating among them. They look forward to hearing the details of your expedition.

"There are evening get-togethers in the meetinghouse." By a wave of his hand, he directed their attention to the glass-fronted building with a wide white door. "Busy get acquainted days for you ahead, Jal.

"Sammie and Bea are participants on occasion and know everyone. Affirm it for me, Bea?"

"I do," Bea replied, "and a most friendly crew they are. Don't worry, Jal; we'll be at the gatherings when our work permits."

Jal reached for Sammie's hand as Bea brushed his face with her wings, "Okay, I won't whine."

Sammie squeezed his fingers a moment or two. "My friend."

Grandfather Moutyn stopped by a cream-colored stone building. "This is the school for academic studies, Jal. You will meet your teacher and fellow students in the morning. But a week's break is on order for you to get acquainted with the village and its folks.

"Today, Tyhe fancies an introduction; he is staying in his guest quarters tonight. Eli is stopping by for dinner and is to spend the evening with us. He must then be elsewhere to finish an assignment. But we can congratulate him on a gripping one completed."

Bea and Sammie glanced at Grandfather Moutyn, and smiled in complicity.

"It's the dinner hour, and everyone scatters to their edibles at this time. That's why we don't see anyone on the streets. A substantial number of residents live in our village, as you can see by the size—increased by one as of today."

Grandfather Moutyn took a seat on a bench and said, "Now, Jal, you mentioned a question? Ask me whatever you wish."

Jal regarded him with somber eyes. "Please, I want to know if you've received a message from Mom and Dad and Uncle Joulh."

"Not today, my lad. However, tomorrow will bring the good news you long for. The report came an hour before you arrived."

Jal beamed at Bea and Sammie.

"Thank you, Grandfather Moutyn. Thank you, a thousand thanks."

"And a thousand welcomes to you, Jal. Let's wend our way home. Aunt Letty prepared her specialty and hankers for our presence at dinner. We don't want to disappoint her."

26

Retracing their steps, they entered the house to the sound of voices coming from the dining room. Jal froze in the doorway, stunned by the being standing at the table conversing with Eli. Tall and regal in appearance, he was dressed in black from head to foot, a black so dark it had a sheen of midnight blue. His piercing black eyes and hooked nose gave his face a stern expression. Tyhe and Eli shook hands with Grandfather Moutyn and saluted Bea and Sammie.

Eli excused himself and smiled with amused eyes as he passed the astonished Jal in the doorway.

Tyhe said in a deep voice, "Who is this? Come here, youngster, and let me look at you. Never fear, I don't eat boys." He ho-hoed loudly. Jal moved toward him warily. "Within a short time, you'll be talking and laughing with Tyhe, won't he, Grandfather Moutyn?"

"Yes, he will. No doubt about it," he replied.

"Don't mind Tyhe's teasing, Jal," Aunt Letty said as she delivered a steaming dish of vegetables to the table.

Dottie, back from her errand, came into the room. She was pretty and slender, with a heart-shaped face framed in chestnut-colored hair. She set out bread, fresh from the oven, and said, "Hello, Sammie. A nifty addition you've brought us. Thanks are in order."

"Bea, I stocked up on packets and pieces of news for our prattling session. Designs for the pink shoes you want are on my desk. This curly haired lad is Jal?" She gave him a hug.

"Mattie is learning to set the table," she said and we're on naperies today.

"Put the napkins like this, Mattie." She illustrated by placing one by the side of a plate.

Aunt Letty asked everybody to sit while she went out and brought in a dumpling stew with an herbal fragrance. Mattie poured milk for Jal and fruit drinks in the other glasses.

Jal took a seat between Bea with her nectar and Sammie with his grains. Their impending separation loomed in his mind, overriding all else. Aunt Letty glanced at Grandfather Moutyn with eyes of sympathy. Soon enough, he would part from his friends, if only temporarily.

Eli came in and took his place on the right of Grandfather Moutyn. *His tawny golden suit is a fitting match for him, as Mel and Cal's outfits were for them,* Jal decided. *Proper dress for kings and warriors,* he said to himself. For a moment, he felt the strength of goodness exuding from Eli and smiled at him. Jal considered everyone at the table, letting his gaze go from one to the other. He glanced at Aunt Letty, who was beaming at him with a dish in her outstretched hand.

He took a portion and said, "It's delicious, thank you, Aunt Letty." He listened as Tyhe, Eli, and Grandfather Moutyn spoke of the activities in the village. They alluded to a cooperative mission they were to execute within six weeks. Bea and Sammie would be on standby assigned to minor tasks, per Syntee's advice.

After dinner, Bea said to Jal and Sammie, "No peeking at my shoes until I wear them at Ben's wedding. Like Jal's mom, I want them to be a surprise."

"We'll be tickled pink to see the itty-bitty shoes. Won't we, Sammie?"

"Absolutely, pink we are." he replied.

"You're incorrigible old fogies, the both of you," she said as she disappeared into Dottie's room.

"An enduring interest of Bea's," Sammie remarked, "modes of dress."

The others met in the courtyard in a broad open space with living quarters on the four sides. Tyhe invited Jal to sit by his side. Undecided, Jal appealed to Sammie with eyes of entreaty, but at his urging, he moved to the seat by Tyhe.

Tyhe said, "Atta boy! We're going to be good friends in short order."

The dialogue streaming round him served as ambient music to Jal's thoughts. He sat, reflecting on his journey, its beginning and ending. His eyes dwelt on the kind and cheerful face of Sammie, so very dear to him. His gaze moved on to the other faces gathered in the courtyard, each one unique, and all expressing radiant goodwill. He recalled the words of Syntee, who had sent him to this home. "I am the Keeper of those who hear and obey my voice."

Jal had a growing sense of wonderment as he listened to the swelling conversation. *Like the stream,* he thought. His journey and the two friends who had brought him here occupied his thoughts until the twilight fell in a blue haze. A change in the tempo of the voices seeped into his awareness. Bea and Dottie had come into the group. He sat content, centered in the hum of the chatter around him.

Soon after moonrise, the gathering ended. Eli would travel to his lodgings to arbitrate his unresolved case on the morrow. Bea pointed to a dark blue door in a row of cabin-like structures that opened on the courtyard. "Tyhe's home whenever he's visiting Grandfather Moutyn, Jal. A diversity of visitors stay here as guests and have a specific color of door. I'm sure you'll soon be meeting most of them."

"Jal, I'll call in shortly," Eli said at leave taking.

Grandfather Moutyn and Tyhe excused themselves. "Tyhe and I have some work we must get through tonight. We'll talk tomorrow, Jal. Goodnight, Bea and Sammie. We'll keep you updated on our plans," he said affably and then re-entered the house with Tyhe.

Upstairs, Jal insisted that Sammie and Bea come into his room.

"Wait," he said. "Stay here." He washed up, brushed his teeth, and dressed in his pajamas. He got into bed and pulled the covers to his chin.

"We'll leave early in the morning after breakfast," Bea said softly. "We need to be home with Syntce before nightfall."

"A shortcut, I presume. I learned that word from Mom. 'Now don't presume Jal,' she'd tell me when I'd say to her, 'I know you'll let me stay the night with Uhlin.'"

"Yes, a shortcut," Sammie said, smoothing Jal's cowlick. "One we use often."

"I'll try not to be too maudlin at your leaving. Dad said to me when I was six years old, 'Now, don't be maudlin, Jal. Suspend the boohoos. I'm only going on a short business trip. Help your mom out while I'm gone.'"

Bea and Sammie lovingly tucked his blanket about him and went to their rooms.

Jal fell asleep promptly and into a dream more remarkable than any encounter of his extraordinary journey. He was never to ascertain afterwards whether it had been a dream or an actual occurrence.

He and Tyhe were soaring upward, higher and higher into the heavens. He clung fast to Tyhe, who spread his great wings and flew swifter than the wind. The stars unfolded in a dazzling panoply of splendor against a gossamer sky. The landscape in a moonlit glow unrolled below him in panoramic brilliance.

"Look, Jal, upon the world at war. See what is and what will be," Tyhe said in a voice that rumbled like thunder.

They flew over desolate wastes scarred by war, vast blots upon the land. Mountains were leveled, as if colossal quakes and volcanoes had shifted the terrain and flipped it upside down. Hills were flattened, and shorn trees lay upended and broken on the ground. Massive hulks of rusting weapons littered the bleak and barren landscape. Colossal rivers and oceans flashed by, and the earth appeared bereft of living beings. And then, when it seemed the whole world was empty and forsaken, the scenes began to change.

"What is and what will be," Tyhe uttered again in the same rumbling tone.

Tree-clad mountains, green, rolling hills, and grassland became visible. Clear streams ran through glades and valleys. The creatures of the woods and birds of the air were full of activity in their varied environments. Multitudes of inhabitants, engaged in harmonious labor, filled magnificent cities and humble villages and countrysides of flourishing farms.

A tableau appeared in which a dark-haired young man was striding through a village. His walk was purposeful, and the residents, busy about their work, stopped to greet him on every side. An older man smiled and lifted his hand in a well-remembered greeting. A man and a woman of mid-age stood at a window observing his movements with eyes of love and pride. A dark-haired young woman gazed after him with a tender light in her eyes. Somehow, the village and the figures were familiar. Busy rummaging through his memories he was interrupted by the voice of Tylie.

"Look and learn, Jal. Keep what you have seen in your heart, for it will surely come to pass. Time to move on."

Jal felt the wind on his face and the swish of the wind in his hair as they began to descend. He was next aware of his bed under him. He grasped his pillow, rolled over, and fell into a deep and dreamless sleep.

Eighth Morning

27

Jal awoke to the voice of Bea perched on his pillow. "Time to get up, Jal. Sammie and I have to be on our way."

Jal pulled the sheet over his face to hide his tears. "Now, now. Remember—maudlin. None of that, or I'll be blubbering. You don't want me to drown in our tears, do you? It won't be long until we see each other again. You can send a message to us by Eli; he stays over on a regular basis. His guest quarters are here, as I told you last night.

"Sammie and I are part of your life. You can't shake us loose from this time forward. For in this country, we're lifelong friends. We'll emigrate to Syntee's homeland in good time; that is, each of us in turn. But even then, we'll only be parted a trifling amount of time. And Jal, it's the greatest fabutale of all—a true one. We'll live happily ever after. Come, let's nip downstairs now with our usual panache."

Jal showered and dressed while she waited for him. Sammie came to the door, and they descended the stairs together.

"The breakfast club has long awaited your arrival," Tyhe said as they entered the dining room.

Bea said, "A tad of bother, please excuse our lateness."

"No bother at all," Aunt Letty replied. "Tyhe likes to tease. Please take your seats and never mind him."

Jal regarded Tyhe with diffidence. His dream during the night seemed tangible, a vibrant reality. *A dream; it had to be a dream!* he thought, and then he sat down between Bea and Sammie. His mind was in such a tangle that the food tasted insipid and bland. Midway through the meal, he let go of his thoughts. *I'll add it to my memory stash on reflections.*

The lively interchange arrested his attention. He focused on the conversation while he gazed at Bea and Sammie. *They're off to their work and had better go home to Syntee.* The thought was absent the usual twinge of pain. *I'm glad I'm not alone anymore,* he said to himself. An onrush of gladness coursed through him; he looked at Bea, then at Sammie, and his face lit up with a smile. Instantly the chatter ceased and everyone spoke in unison, "Welcome home, Jal."

Jal and Grandfather Moutyn walked with Bea and Sammie to the outskirts of the village. Once more on the familiar path that would lead them home, Sammie paused at the bridge.

"Be sure to keep your hair dry, Bea," Jal called out to her. She stood up and blew him a kiss as a beam of light separated and opened like a door. Sammie stepped through, and the beam of light closed behind them.

Filled with wonder, Jal began to launch into questions. Grandfather Moutyn gently laid his hand on his shoulder. "In good time all will be known, my dear boy. At present, the day gives fair promise and awaits our attendance. Revelations are in-flight and due to make a prompt landing."

Content to wait, Jal cached his questions in certainty of future answers. In sure anticipation, he and Grandfather Moutyn turned their steps homeward.

Acknowledgments

My thanks to those who read and reviewed this work in progress: Bob, Barbara, Carol, Dawn, Lisa, and Joan Williams, in particular. Your encouragement motivated me throughout the writing of this book.

A thank you to the Blue Ridge Writer's Group, who in one brief meeting scuttled my sense of ease and scurried me on to the hard task of revising, editing, revising, editing, ad infinitum.

To Morgan, Chelsea and Jayne, my aspirants, press on and write great books.

About the Author

Nancy Janes, a former Clinical Social Worker, lives in the Blue Ridge Mountains of North Carolina. She finds the life stories and cultures of others inspiring and leans toward assorted genres of literary and non-literary books.

A series of stories to follow? "Wait and see," as our narrative advises.

CPSIA information can be obtained at www.ICGtesting.com
Printed in the USA
LVOW10s1610230913

353729LV00016B/620/P